## A TRUE STORY
### as told by the stowaway Harry Naughton

# OLYMPIAD V
## The 1912 Stockholm Games

HARRY
NAUGHTON

POP
WARNER

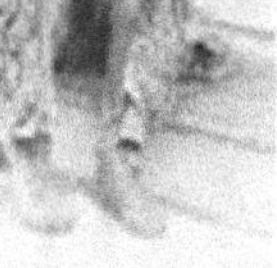

the stowaway

the coach

GEORGE
PATTON

JIM
THORPE

DUKE
KAHANAMOKU

the athletes

"AMERICANS ALL"

# OLYMPIAD V
## by
## HARRY NAUGHTON
## THE FANTASTICALLY TRUE STORY OF THE 1912 UNITED STATES OLYMPIC TEAM AS TOLD BY THE STOWAWAY HARRY NAUGHTON

# A VERY GOOD PLACE TO START

Well, I reckoned I would write this down as it was still fresh in my mind, see'in as lots of things gets changed around and prettied up as time goes by. Mostly folks are wantin to paint a better picture of themselves to show they was more noble, or truthful, or did the right thing, when maybe they did nothin or the wrong thing. Now, I'm not one to put on the white wig and commence passin out judgement on anyone as I'm guilty of stretchin the facts to fit the truth as much as the next fool. But my aim here is to tell it like I seen it, without tryin to make myself out the hero, or show that I done bettern I did, which in my opinion, is the Grandaddy of all lies.

I know that you'all are itchin to hear about the Olympics and the Gold medals and the Glory and meetin the King of Sweden and his missus the Queen and how I saved the day and we'll sure enough get around to that. But just like in church when they tell a story from the Bible and you know the ending cuz you've heard it a thousand times, such as when David whipped up on the Giant with a river rock and then cut off his head and paraded it all around the town and got to marry the Kings daughter, this story has a beginning and an end, with a lot of excitin bits in between.

I guess my story starts in Toledo when I was borned, but I were'nt in no condition to remember exactly what happened. People that wuz there, said I done alright and didn't put up too much of a fuss. Other than fishin and trampin around, one of the first things I clearly recall, is the day my Daddy got kilt down at the sawmill. They brought him to the house bundled up on a 2x12 plank, gave my Ma a twenty dollar gold piece for her troubles said "Sorry" and left. Mama laid down, right on the kitchen floor and didn't get up, ceptin to go to the funeral, for nigh on a year. Then one day she just got goin and things was back to normal for a spell, until Mr. Stiller started comin around, courtin.

Mr. Stiller was a widower with three good sized boys that he said needed a mothers touch. The general concensus of the citizenry however, was that they was in need of a lion tamer or somethin more permanent like hangin.

Mr. Stiller had set his sights on my Ma and thats what he got, and then some. That my sisters and me was part of the bargain seemed of little consequence, him bein the foreman at the textile mill and we was of an age to work. And so we did. From six in the mornin till four in the evenin, Monday thru Saturday, with Christmas day and the Fourth of July off, to rest up.

For a long time there wer'nt no trouble down at the mill, then some folks up in Washington D. C. pestered President Taft to chop down the work week from sixty hours to fiftyfour and not let younguns work at all. Which was not as popular an idea as President Taft might have guessed. It didn't make no sense at all for a girl child to go to school and it was easier to whistle a rattlesnake into a bottle than get boys who had been makin a mans wages to go back, so the whole affair was just hard feelin's and bloodshed and nobody come away satisfied.

I had worked the mill since I was ten and knew ever nut and bolt and which way to turn em in the whole danged place. I knew where to have a smoke or catch forty winks without anybody the wiser and figured I would work there until I died. Lot's of people had. That's why it come as a surprise when my step daddy called me into his office and tole me he had sold the mill and the whole family was moving to Detroit. Now I didn't know where Detroit was but I figured it must be off over in Europe somewheres as Mr. Stiller was always goin on about how grand it was on the continent and such.

I shoulda waited to ask but it was the first thing on my mind and then it was on my tongue and I just spit it out. I said, "Can I take Pluck?" Pluck was my dog. I had raised her mama from a pup and she had had a hard time with the last litter and died, Pluck bein the only survivor. Hence the name. Not so much lucky as plucky. Her sire was of the English pit bull variety, with beady little eyes and a long pointy snout which made her look a whole lot meaner than what she was, her demeanor bein more in the fraidy cat line than bull baiter.

Experience has since taught me, that it's always better to beg forgivness than ask permission, but I was just fifteen and held a much higher opinion of our species then, than I do today .Mr. Stiller didn't miss a beat and tole me straightout that there was no lack of dogs in Detroit and I would have to "Shoot the damn dog." end of conversation. I would sooner have shot the town barber as Pluck so, I figured it was of a season for me to move on. Bein pert near full growed, I aimed to make my way in the world.

As it seemed the whole nation was on fire to head West, I figured to beat the rush and go East. I had seen pitchers of New York City and heard tell of an indoors circus there that ran day and night, with no end of clowns and fire eaters and such. I had a chunk of money saved up that I felt would last me ten or twenty years if I was thrifty and didn't eat too much, so I said my goodbyes to my sisters and my Ma. Tellin her I was goin to see relations on my daddy's side, I bought a ticket on the train to Pittsburg, Pennsylvania

Now I don't generally recommend tellin lies, even little white ones to your Ma. But if I had tole her I was headed to New York to the circus and whatever other mischief there was to be had there, it would've broke her heart. What she didn't know, for sure couldn't hurt her, so I done it. I'm sorry for it now and wished I hadn't. I would have apologized proper and promised never to do it agin if she'd of lived, but she caught a fever and died afore I got back, so I never got the oppurtunity.

Takin the train was the first time I had been more than ten miles outside of Toledo. Bein a world traveler was just grand, settin up in the passenger car, wearin my Sunday clothes and watchin the world roll by my window. There was Nigra porters that had'ta bring whatever you wanted. And if it wasn't just right or to your liking, say if your tea was too hot or too cold, they would take it back and bring you a new one until it was.

I got as far as Cleveland before thinkin I could ride for free in the box cars. I seen other fellas doin it and other than gettin a mite dirty it seemed like a good way to conserve my finances. I collected my luggage, cashed in my ticket and slunk around, until the train to New York headed out.

I had befriended a fellow traveler, Artemus Hitchins of Charleston, South Carolina. A boy of about my age and size but far more s'perienced with the particulars of "ridin the rails." Most of which involved not gettin throwed under the wheels and keepin a sharp eye out for the yard Bulls, whose job it was to knock you in the head and throw you off for not havin' a ticket. We waited till the train started rollin, then went for the first boxcar that looked empty with an open door. Artemus ran hard alongside and threw his bag up and in, then grabbed a hold of the ladder and flipped hisself into the car. I did the same, feelin pretty pleased with myself for not gettin kilt or worse. As we were congratulatin each other, our eyes got adjusted to the dimness of the car and Artemus stopped talkin all of a sudden. A hard look had come over his face. There was four Nigra men loungin and sittin' against the back of the car. "We got to get off." he says "I ain't ridin with no niggers. Come on" and out goes his bag and him after it.

I knew he was right and that I shoud have jumped too, but I was still in the glow of bein in one piece and on the train so I held back. I had known many coloreds workin back at the mill and they always seemed to know their place and treat a white man with the proper respect, so I just tole those nigras that I was a goin to stay just the same and to pay me no mind. Just then little Pluck nosed her way out of my travel bag and barked hello. They all grinned and made us welcome, so I had a smoke and settled in for the ride to New York.

In the summer of 1912, Jim Crow was the law of the land and there was plenty of ways for a nigra to get on the wrong side of it. A black man could not be seen talking to a white woman after dark and had to make way for even the trashiest of white men. This seemed right. Thats just how things was and always would be. Just one drop of black blood was enough to shade a person and mark them and their children and grandchildren forever. Injuns, chinee, eskimo It don't make no difference. To be caught drawing water from the white mans well so to speak, was a guaranteed invite to your own necktie party.

Now these coloreds I had throwed in with on the train was nice enough fellers and let me have the best corner and sang hymns and played with Pluck and taught her some tricks. I gave each of them a penny so they wouldn't think about stealin anything for a week or two, and when it came time to quit the train they jumped out aways ahead of me so I wouldn't be seen keepin their company. Nice fellers all around.

New York City was bigger and dirtier than anything I could have imagined. And the commotion! There was not one minute of peace. Like when the mill was running at top speed, or a cicada bug that just hums and hums with no end to it. I asked where the circus was but they tole me that what I wanted was the Vaudville and that I would have to get cleaned up some before they would let me in as I was black as a beetle from the train. And no dogs allowed, lessen you was blind.

What I wanted was a room, with a bed and a sink to wash up. For a man of means such as myself, this was no problem. I took a buggy to a hotel near Broadway and hiding Pluck in my bag, rented a room for the night. I fell hard asleep and was resurrected by the bell of a streetcar outside my window just after dark. With my clothes cleaned and my hair slicked back, I was ready to "paint the town". Leaving Pluck in the room with my bag, I took just enough money for the evening and hid the rest under my mattress.

The Vaudville was sure enough a circus, but there wern't no Pacyderms or Zebras or a ringmaster as usual. Clowns though, they had em for days. Jugglers and gymnasts and pool sharks for sure and one clown got swatted with a board called a slapstick that exploded and scared the whole place for a minute or two. It was just grand. But after eight hours or so they started repeatin the acts and I knew all the jokes and there wern't no more surprises, so I give it up and headed back to my room at the hotel. On the way I even paid a nickel to go inside a tent and see the tattooed lady. She was awful pretty, but had kind of a sour face like she had et something that was still undecided on which way it was goin to go.

I figured Pluck would be powerful hungry by now, so I got a bone from the butcher and wrapped it in some newsprint so's I could sneak it past the desk clerk. That went all right and I was feelin pretty smart about the whole experience of leavin home until I got to my room. As I stood there in the hallway with the key in one hand and a soup bone in the other, I seen that my door was open just a crack. "Hello!" I says. No reply. No barkin neither. "Pluck!", I hollered."Pluck!!" Nothin. Keepin that bone at the ready, I went on in. It looked like a tornado had come through there and turned everything inside out. Robbed. Everything I owned was gone. Gone. No money, no clothes and no dog. I ain't ashamed to admit it, I sat down right there and begin to bawl. Cried my eyes out. Tole myself that my life was over and I could just lay down right then and there and give up the ghost. Bein pert near wore out from the travel and the excitement and the exertion of feelin sorry for myself, I cried myself to sleep.

The mornin' came quick and hard with the innkeeper poundin on the door sayin pay up or git out. I tole him what had happened but he didn't seem all that surprised, just said he warn't runnin' no church and how was I figurin' on payin for the damage to the room. All I had left in the world was what was on my back. And all I could think was that I was hungry, homeless, pissed off, tired and broke and needed to find my dog. So I lit out of there with him a yellin after me and hit the bricks with no thought but to try and find Pluck.

INT. WINGED FIST IRISH ATHLETIC CLUB – NEW YORK CITY – 1912

The hall is standing room only packed with athletes and supporters from across the nation, many meeting for the first time. Colonel Thompson, James Sullivan and other dignitaries command the stage.

REAR ADMIRAL RICHARD WAINRIGHT

Ladies and gentlemen. Before I introduce our esteemed President of the Olympic committee, (cheers from the crowd) allow me to state, that although my days of athletic prowess are behind me, I still possess a mighty voice and plan to lose it, cheering you on to victory at Stockholm. (cheers) Without further adieu, I give you our leader and benefactor, Colonel Robert Means Thompson. (louder whistles, catcalls and cheering)

COLONEL THOMPSON

Let me give it to you straight from the shoulder boys. We are going over to Stockholm, not as sports, but as sportsmen. We are going to show the representatives of the forty nations against whom we compete, that we can take defeat with victory,..and prove to the world,... that composite though we are, our ancestors made no mistake in forging this great nation. (cheers) I want to say, that I am proud to lead you all. I want to feel that I'll have reasons to be prouder still when we return triumphant from these great games. (cheers) Tonight, you will be issued uniforms and berth assignments aboard our ship the Finland. Tomorrow, the invasion commences. (cheers) I ask that you keep in mind, you represent the United States both on and off the athletic field. I exhort you to embody the spirit of past Olympians in

your endeavors. Faster,... (cheers) higher,... (cheers) stronger...
(crescendo of cheers)

DISSOLVE TO:

EXT. NEW YORK CITY JUNE 1912 – MORNING

A young boy, making his way through the back alleys and side streets of New York City, hears the muted strains of a marching band. As he approaches a main thoroughfare, cheering crowds pack the sidewalks, preventing him from pushing through to the front. He spies a lamp post and climbs. From his vantage point above the crowd he views a procession of uniformed young men and women in loose formation, smiling and waving through a blizzard of confetti. Somewhat confused, he calls out to a man standing on the sidewalk just below.

HARRY

(shouting) Who're we fight'in?

BYSTANDER

(shouting) What?

HARRY

(louder) Who're we fight'in?

BYSTANDER

(shouting) Nobody, it's the Olympics

HARRY

(shouting) What's a Olympics?

BYSTANDER

(shouting) Can you read?

HARRY

(nodding yes) Some

The bystander takes a copy of the New York Times from under his arm and passes it up to Harry, then turns his attention back to the parade. Athletically securing his position on the lamppost by wrapping one leg around, Harry opens the paper to see the headline "OLYMPIC ATHLETES SHOW GREAT FORM – INDIANS WIN" Slowly mouthing the words as he reads, the name Jim Thorpe catches his eye and he expectantly scans the uniformed athletes for a familiar face.

With the end of the parade approaching, Harry shimmies down the pole and moves into the street, deftly sidestepping a trail of road apples. Joining the attendant crush of people, he is swept towards the harbor where five thousand flag waving well wishers surround the beribboned transatlantic steamship Finland. Pandemonium prevails as the parade approaches, the arrival of the Olympic team dangerously overcrowding the dock and disrupting final preparations for departure. Off to one side, a group of delinquent boys tie a string of firecrackers onto the tail of a puppy and laughing, send it howling into the crowd. Frightened, one of a half dozen cavalry horses balks at being led onto the ship and breaks free from it's handler, threatening to maim or kill as it makes it's escape. Quick as lightning, one of the Olympic athletes jumps in front of the horse. Spreading his arms wide the animal rears up, hooves flailing. Fearlessly, he grabs the loose halter and hangs on. Firecrackers are still popping as Harry breaks free from the frightened crowd and calls to the pup.

HARRY (CONT'D)S

(shouting) Pluck!.. Pluck! Come here girl! Come here!

Harry throws his coat over the terrified puppy and pulling it close to his chest, puts out the firecrackers. Looking up, Harry realizes that the uniformed athlete is his hero, All American, Jim Thorpe. Jim, having calmed the wild eyed horse, effortlessly swings astride and giving Harry a nod, rides along the dock to appreciative applause amidst the pop and flash of cameras, until confronted by a red faced cavalry officer.

LIEUTENANT GEORGE PATTON

(FORCEFULLY) DISMOUNT! DISMOUNT, DAMN YOU!

Patton immediately seizes the horses bridle, locking eyes with the bareback rider as he issues the command. Jim, completely relaxed and in his element as the center of attention, smiles down at the upset officer, the halter rope loose in his hands.

THORPE

(casually) Sure thing Captain. You're welcome.

Gracefully, Thorpe swings his leg over the neck of the horse landing softly next to Patton, then hands him the halter rope.

THORPE (CONT'D)

You boys ought to keep a closer watch over your livestock. Somebody could have got their feelin's hurt.

A group of officers and other members of the Olympic team has gathered around the two men, adding to the already tense situation. Patton, livid now and running his hands over the foreleg of the horse addresses Thorpe indirectly.

LIEUTENANT PATTON

You damn savage! If this animal is injured in any way, I'll see you in irons, after I beat some sense into you.

Thorpe, still relaxed but appraising the situation.
THORPE

Any time you're feeling froggy Custer, just jump.

Patton, unable to believe what he has just heard, jerks upright, his riding crop raised to deliver a blow. Thorpe however, has pivoted and is now standing to the side of Patton, the bright morning sun to his back. A commanding male voice freezes the interaction.
COLONEL THOMPSON

(forcefully) Stand down sir! We'll have none of that!

Patton and his men snap to attention as the superior officer takes charge of the situation. Thorpe, still in a defensive posture, waits.
COLONEL THOMPSON (CONT'D)

Lieutenant, see that this animal gets aboard without further incident.

LIEUTENANT PATTON

Yes sir.

COLONEL THOMPSON

(addressing the Olympic team) The rest of you, gather your kit and get on this ship. We sail within the hour. Thorpe, I need a word with you.

Pulling Jim aside Colonel Thompson queries him.
THORPE

(respectfully) Sir?

COLONEL THOMPSON

What was all that about?

THORPE

(shrugging) The horse got loose, I brought her back. End of
story.

As they are speaking together, a stocky, purposeful looking man,
dressed in civilian clothes and smoking a cigar strides towards them.
COLONEL THOMPSON

(shaking hands) Mr. Warner, seems we're off to a shaky start.

POP WARNER

(rapidly) I saw the whole thing Colonel. For Chrissake, Jim's
a hero! That officer was completely out of line.

COLONEL THOMPSON

Lieutenant Patton, one of our best. Stands to medal in the
games... Just be thankful he's on our side. Now, time is short
and no harm done, let's get aboard and save the fireworks for
Stockholm shall we?

POP WARNER

Right you are sir... Come on Jim, the wars over.

THORPE

Wouldn't have been much of a scalp any ways Coach.

POP WARNER

Hummph!

DISSOLVE TO:

EXT. FORT MEYERS VIRGINIA MAY 1912 – DAY

A hotly contested Polo match is underway. One player stands out on the U.S. Cavalry team. Playing rough and using rougher language, he manages to score when it seems impossible.

CAPTAIN FRANK MCCOY

There's your man. On the big bay.

COLONEL THOMPSON

Patton? No doubt he's a fine horseman. Can he run.. shoot?

CAPTAIN FRANK MCCOY

Crack shot with a pistol. Absolute devil with the sabre and swims like a fish. Still holds the 200 meter record in the high hurdles at West Point. Rumor has it he was raised by savages until he was twelve. Can't spell worth a damn though.

COLONEL THOMPSON

Their are no medals for spelling at the games Captain.

CAPTAIN FRANK MCCOY

Sir.

COLONEL THOMPSON

What's the chink in his armor Frank? His Achilles heel?

CAPTAIN FRANK MCCOY

That would be his mouth sir.

COLONEL THOMPSON

Come again?

CAPTAIN FRANK MCCOY

Can't keep the thing shut. He's both opinionated and profane. I've heard him use language that would make Bluebeard blush.

COLONEL THOMPSON

Is he the best we've got?

CAPTAIN FRANK MCCOY

Absolutely. No one else comes close.

COLONEL THOMPSON

Well..See if you can't have the barb removed from his foot. That way if he sticks it in his mouth we can get it out.

CAPTAIN FRANK MCCOY

I know just the surgeon sir.

COLONEL THOMPSON

We have less than sixty days to the start of the games in Stockholm. Including two weeks aboard ship. Can he be ready?

Patton holds his polo mallet in the air after scoring as his teammates and spectators cheer wildly.

CAPTAIN FRANK MCCOY

Appears he's ready now Colonel.

INT. CAPTAIN MCCOYS OFFICE

Colonel Thompson and Captain McCoy are seated as 2nd Lieutenant Patton enters, still muddy from the polo match. Patton comes to attention and snaps a perfect salute.

LIEUTENANT PATTON

Reporting as ordered. Sir.

CAPTAIN FRANK MCCOY

At ease Lieutenant...Introductions are in order. George, this is Colonel Thompson.

(shaking hands) Seems they're having a little party in Stockholm in a couple months and the Colonel was wondering if you would like to attend.

LIEUTENANT PATTON

My calender is open Colonel.

COLONEL THOMPSON

Lieutenant, have you heard of the modern Olympic games?

(Patton nods yes) The founder, a Frenchman, Baron Pierre Cubertain has created a competition consisting of five events. A modern Pentathlon, conceived to test the fitness of the perfect man at arms of the present day. Skills that would be necessary should a courier find himself in jeopardy behind enemy lines. Pistol marksmanship at twenty-five meters, fencing...a swim of three hundred meters...a five thousand meter steeple chase, on an unfamiliar mount and a cross country run of four thousand meters.

LIEUTENANT PATTON

Sounds like a long day Colonel.

COLONEL THOMPSON

(laughing) The events will be held over a five to ten day period with adequate time to rest. We sail from New York mid June, with the games commencing in early July. You would be the sole representative of the armed forces of the United States at the games. Can you be ready?

LIEUTENANT PATTON

With the Captains permission, I can be ready within the hour sir.

COLONEL THOMPSON

That's the spirit!

Captain McCoy brings a crystal decanter and three glasses to his desk.

CAPTAIN FRANK MCCOY

Permission granted. A toast then. To victory at Stockholm! The three touch glasses.

ALL

Victory!

DISSOLVE TO:

EXT. NEW YORK HARBOR – DAY

Harry and Pluck rejoin the parade, continuing along the dock, up the gang plank and onto the Finland.

Seeing that no one is paying any attention to him, he finds a perfect place to rest in one of the extra lifeboats stored on deck in response to the recent Titanic tragedy.

HARRY

We'll just hole up here for a spell Pluck, get our wits about us and see what comes. Hush now. That's my girl.

The send off festivities continue, good byes are said, all ashore is sounded and eventually the Finland casts off, her rails lined with passengers and Olympic hopefuls catching a last glimpse of the New York City skyline.

CUT TO:

EXT DECK OF THE STEAMSHIP FINLAND – MORNING

With baggage in tow, members of the Olympic team show boarding passes to various stewards who direct them to their quarters. Ultimately, black athlete Howard Drew, Hawaiian swimmer Duke Kahanamoku, and native American track and field stars Jim Thorpe, Lewis Tewanina and Andrew Sokalexis are directed forward to one cabin in third class.

INT. THIRD CLASS CABIN ABOARD THE FINLAND – DAY

Thorpe, Andrew and Lewis are the last to arrive finding Duke, and Howard already settling in.

THORPE

Well, what a surprise. I thought for sure I'd be bunking with
the Captain. I'll check with the porter and see if there's been
a mistake.

Laughter all around as Thorpe chucks his bag onto an empty bunk.
THORPE (CONT'D)

Howard! I thought you'd be in with the rest of the Winged
Fists. Or are you not Irish anymore?

HOWARD DREW

Oh, I'm Irish all right. I just have to stay down here in the
dark with you feller's for a spell, see if I can't lose some of this
Philadelphia tan.

THORPE

(shaking hands all around, Thorpe comes last to Duke) Names Jim. What tribe are you from bud? I'm pretty sure you're with the right bunch, I just never seen an Injun with a pair of choppers like what you got.

Sporting a huge grin, showcasing his perfect white teeth, Duke introduces himself.

DUKE

(smiling) Howzit! I'm Duke.

THORPE

(bowing deeply) Well... excuse ME, your majesty. Shouldn't you be up in first class with the rest of the quality?

DUKE

(laughing) It was my Dad's name. He was born when the Duke of England visited Hawaii.

THORPE

Hawaii? I heard about that somewhere's. You the boys that do the fire dancing?

DUKE

(smiling) Some do. I do my dancing in the water.

THORPE

There's plenty around. You might just get a chance to do some dancin' yet.

Lewis has lain down on the floor, obviously not feeling well.
THORPE (CONT'D)

Maybe you can give Lewis some lessons. Appears he's a land lubber after all.

More laughter all around as Lewis groans, pulling a pillow over his head.
INT. DARKENED HULL OF LIFEBOAT – NIGHT
Harry, the reality of what he has done sinking in, shares what little food he has with the pup.
HARRY

(whispering) Well Pluck, we're in it now. There's no turnin' back. We'll just hold on and see what the mornin' brings.

Crying softly, the now quiet ship and constant thrum of the engines lull him to sleep.
INT. SAWMILL TOLEDO, OHIO – DAY
Harry is working the line with older men and young children in a ballet of efficiency. The dust and noise are overwhelming.
FOREMAN MILLER

(shouting) Harry!! Harry!!

Harry gives a nod and taps the man alongside him on the shoulder, letting him know he is leaving the line.
HARRY

Whats shakin' Davy?

FOREMAN MILLER

Old man Stiller wants you up in the office.

HARRY

You mean my new Pa?

FOREMAN MILLER

On his best day, he'll never be half the man your Pa was.

HARRY

Don't I know it.

FOREMAN MILLER

Best shake a leg now.

HARRY

Thanks Davy

Harry moves through the mill, smiling and gesturing to every worker he encounters.

INT. MR. STILLERS OFFICE – DAY

Harry enters the office and greets the receptionist who is in tears.

HARRY

Hey sis...Whoa! What's wrong?

MOLLY NAUGHTON

Oh Harry, It's just awful. Why can't things just be like they used to.

HARRY

What's happened?

An interior door opens and a balding man with a drooping mustache sticks his head out his office door.

MR. STILLER

All right! Stop that bawlin'! Harry get in here. Now.

Molly waves him in and buries her tear stained face in a handkerchief.

Mr. Stiller straightens his coat and takes his seat behind the desk.

HARRY

Just what's got her all worked up?

MR. STILLER

Watch your tone boy.

HARRY

Well?

MR. STILLER

I have sold the mill.

HARRY

And?

MR. STILLER

I am taking the family to Detroit.

HARRY

Just like that?

MR. STILLER

Just like that.

HARRY

What does Ma say?

MR. STILLER

Her wish is that you will accompany us. I am against it.

HARRY

Can I bring Pluck?

MR. STILLER

I seriously doubt there is any shortage of mongrels in Michigan. My advice to you is, shoot the damn dog and be done with it.

HARRY

(shouting) I'd just as soon shoot the Barber.

MR. STILLER

That would simply hasten the inevitable.

HARRY

The what?

MR. STILLER

Your residency.. at the penitentary.

HARRY

You go to hell!!

Harry turns and slams the door on his way out.

DISSOLVE TO:

EXT. UPPER DECK OF THE FINLAND – MORNING

Athletes are working out all over the ship. Every inch of available deck area is utilized, transforming the Finland into a floating gymnasium. Sprinters and hurdlers compete on a cork track. Tethered javelins are thrown into the ocean. The intermittent crack of live pistol fire from the fantail mingling with the shouts and splash of swimmers training in an eight foot square canvas water tank, a rope tied around their waists providing resistance.

Commencing the daily life boat drill, one of the ships officers blows his whistle three times. As several crew members work together to lower a boat, young Harry is rudely awakened and then discovered as the sailors pull back the canvas tarp covering the boat.

SEAMAN JOHNSON

(loudly) Ho now! What's this? Wouldn't happen to have a ticket now would you sonny?

Harry, disheveled and not quite awake shakes his head "no" as several sailors peer into the lifeboat.

SEAMAN JOHNSON (CONT'D)

Do you know what we do to stowaways on this ship?

Frightened now, Harry again shakes his head "no".

SEAMAN JOHNSON (CONT'D)

We puts em in a pot with some potatoes and onions to make a nice stew. Isn't that right boys?

Affirmative grunts from his fellow crew members.
CHIEF PETTY OFFICER MONTAGE

(shouting) Mister Johnson! What's the holdup here?

Seaman Johnson reaches into the lifeboat and pulls out a snarling Pluck by the scruff of her neck.
SEAMAN JOHNSON

Seems we have some nonrevenue passengers aboard sir.

HARRY

Hey you! Let her go!

CHIEF PETTY OFFICER MONTAGE

Take them into custody and get on with the drill. I will inform the captain.

SEAMAN JOHNSON

Aye aye sir!

Handing the squirming pup to another sailor and grabbing Harry by his hair, Seaman Johnson roughly pulls him from the life boat, boxing him about the ears once he is on deck. By now, athletes have gathered from around the ship, their morning workouts interrupted by the discovery of the stowaways. Seaman Johnson, clearly aware of his audience, continues to strike the boy. Raising his hand to deliver yet another blow, he finds it in the grasp of second lieutenant George Patton, who deftly twists it behind the sailors back. Pushing him forward and grabbing a fistful of hair with his free hand, he slams Johnson's face into the ships railing.

LIEUTENANT PATTON

The order was to take him into custody, not beat him to death.

The crowd has easily doubled in size as more athletes and passengers are drawn to the fracas. Growling, the little pup has wriggled free and clamps onto Seaman Johnson's trouser leg while Patton, out of uniform and encircled by Johnson's shipmates, is at an obvious disadvantage.

COLONEL THOMPSON

At ease Lieutenant.

Patton releases the sailor who collapses to the deck. His face bleeding as the attendant sailors snap to attention.

SEAMAN JOHNSON

(angrily) Get this damn dog off me! He had no call to do that Colonel. No call. I was just following orders.

COLONEL THOMPSON

Stand up man.

Harry grabs Pluck before Seaman Johnson pulls himself to his feet then stands at attention.

SEAMAN JOHNSON

Sir.

COLONEL THOMPSON

Report.

SEAMAN JOHNSON

I was discharging my duty sir when this madman attacked me.

Colonel Johnson looks past the seaman to see the boy being cared for by several women passengers, his left eye already swollen from the thrashing.

COLONEL THOMPSON

Lieutenant.

LIEUTENANT PATTON

Sir.

COLONEL THOMPSON

You are free to continue your training.

LIEUTENANT PATTON

(saluting) Sir.

Patton turns and jogs away as Colonel Thompson questions the seaman.

COLONEL THOMPSON

What's the boy done?

SEAMAN JOHNSON

Stowaway sir. It's the brig for him.

A large crowd has gathered, athletes and passengers keenly interested in the goings on. Colonel Thompson walks over to the boy.

COLONEL THOMPSON

What's your name boy?

HARRY

Naughton, Harry Naughton from Toledo sir.

COLONEL THOMPSON

That your pup?

HARRY

Yessir. Her names Pluck.

COLONEL THOMPSON

Aptly named. How come you to be aboard?

HARRY

Well sir, what with the parade and the excitement and all I just wound up here. I wanted to see the Indian and find the Olympics.

COLONEL THOMPSON

The Indian?

HARRY

Yes sir, Thorpe. The footballer.

COLONEL THOMPSON

Where are your folks son?

HARRY

None to speak of sir. I'm my own man now.

Colonel Thompson stands for a moment, all eyes watching him.
COLONEL THOMPSON

Mr. Naughton.

HARRY

Sir?

COLONEL THOMPSON

The one thing this team could use is luck. We have the talent and the will and I believe we have the Lords good favor...

(Speaking to the crowd) I hereby nominate Harry Naughton of Toledo, for the position of team mascot.

Cheers from the surrounding athletes and crowd.
COLONEL THOMPSON (CONT'D)

All in favor say aye.

A resounding shout of Aye!!
COLONEL THOMPSON (CONT'D)

All opposed?

Complete silence from the crowd.

COLONEL THOMPSON (CONT'D)

The ayes have it.

More cheers

COLONEL THOMPSON (CONT'D)

(shaking hands with Harry) Do you accept sir?

Harry nods yes.

COLONEL THOMPSON (CONT'D)

(to the crowd at large) I'll stand for the lads fare. And if it be Gods will... we'll all find the Olympics.

Laughter and more cheers from the crowd. Seaman Johnson draws a finger across his throat and gives Harry a menacing stare before he is dismissed by Colonel Thompson.

PURSER MACDOWELL

Might I have a word with you Colonel?

COLONEL THOMPSON

Of course, What is it?

PURSER MACDOWELL

Seems we're full up Colonel. There's nowhere to put the lad.

COLONEL THOMPSON

Give me just a moment would you. (waving to Pop Warner) Mr. Warner.

POP WARNER

At your service Colonel.

COLONEL THOMPSON

Do you think you might persuade Mr. Thorpe to share a cabin with Mr. Kiviat?

POP WARNER

The Jew? Why?

COLONEL THOMPSON

We need a bunk for Harry here.

POP WARNER

He doesn't mind being put in with the coloreds?

COLONEL THOMPSON

Well Harry?

HARRY

No sir, I don't mind. And Pluck neither. It's got to be a sight more comfortable than that danged boat.

POP WARNER

I'll run it by Jim. I know he'd appreciate having a little more elbow room... Abel's got a cabin to himself?

COLONEL THOMPSON

I believe so.

POP WARNER

That Olympic uniform doesn't fix everything does it Colonel.

COLONEL THOMPSON

It's a beginning Mr. Warner.

POP WARNER

I'll see what I can do.

COLONEL THOMPSON

I would be in your debt sir.

POP WARNER

Consider it done.

INT. THIRD CLASS CABIN ABOARD THE FINLAND
Harry has been berthed with the segregated athletes.
HARRY

(Voiceover) I had been plucked from the frying pan and then from the fire so fast that I can not recommend one over the other. The timely intervention of Lieutenant Patton and Colonel Thompson serving doubly to save both my hide and reputation. The shame of sharing a cabin with the coloreds has been put off considerable by the fact that my hero Jim Thorpe, the Carlise Indian is among us.

HARRY (CONT'D)

Though he is not, as I had first hoped, my constant companion. His fellows have taken me under their wing and I am simmering in a potluck of exotic cultures. I spend most of my time with Duke, him being the closest to me in age. He comes from the Sandwich Islands. I had never heard of them before but he sure makes it sound nice. Say's it's just sun and blue water and warm all the time...even Christmas and there's nothing to do all day but fish and swim and mess around with boats and find shells on the beach. He's got a tiny little guitar called a ukulele and he plays it and sings the sweetest songs you ever heard. Sometimes the song's make me feel a little sad and miss my folks and I get to feelin' sorry for myself but then the next one will pick me right up and we'll all be laughing and clapping and singing along. Ain't it funny how music can do a body that way.

CUT TO:

EXT. UPPER DECK OF THE FINLAND – DAY
(Voiceover)

Up on deck is where the action is and there's plenty of it too. All the boys that ain't seasick are runnin and jumpin and shooting and sword fighting and wrestlin every minute. That is except for Jim. He told me that all he has to do is close his eyes and picture hisself doing whatever it is he wants to do and then when the time comes he just up and does it. And bettern anyone else to boot. I tried it once but I don't think I've quite got the hang of it and aim to put in more practice.

Jim Thorpe reclines in a deck chair as various athletes run past him.

Lazily closing his eyes, he pictures himself running the full length of a football field ,evading all tacklers until he stands in the end zone acknowledging the roar of appreciation from a packed full stadium.

DISSOLVE TO:

EXT. – CARLISE INDIAN SCHOOL FOOTBALL FIELD – DAY

Jim Thorpe and several teammates in soiled football uniforms have finished practice and are headed for the showers.

ALBERT EXIDINE

Just one more game boys and the season is over. What do you think Jim, are you gonna come back next year or what?

JIM THORPE

I dunno, I'm feeling kinda beat up right now, so it could be... or what. We'll see how this knee holds up through the track season.

Pop Warner is speaking with one of his assistants when he looks up and sees Jim and the group walk by.

POP WARNER

(shouting) Thorpe... Thorpe!

Jim looks over his shoulder and makes an incredulous face while pointing at himself and mouthing "Who me?"

POP WARNER

(CONT'D) Yeah you, knucklehead! Come over here for a minute.

Jim heads over to Pop, affecting a limp.

POP WARNER (CONT'D)

You ought to be in pictures with that kind of acting.

JIM THORPE

Don't I know it!

POP WARNER

Is it really bothering you?

JIM THORPE

Not bad. I just like to know you care.

POP WARNER

What I care about is winning the national title. We missed by a cats whisker this year and I think we have a real shot next season.

JIM THORPE

What's the schedule look like. Same?

POP WARNER

Basically... Army's going to be tough. They've got a couple of defensive backs that will be gunning for you. Eisenhower and Bradley.

JIM THORPE

I know that character. "Ike", they call him. I'll burn that bridge when I get to it.

POP WARNER

So you ARE coming back?

JIM THORPE

I didn't say that. There's some money to be made out there, that's for sure. I've had offers..

POP WARNER

What if I told you about something that could double or triple those offers?

JIM THORPE

I'm all ears coach.

POP WARNER

The Olympics.

JIM THORPE

Aren't those kind of a joke?

POP WARNER

Not anymore. They'll be using all the latest electronic timers and what records they have now, I'm pretty sure you could smash. Under my expert tutelage of course.

JIM THORPE

Of course... OK, I'll bite, when and where.

POP WARNER

Stockholm, Sweden, in June. They have a brand new stadium and the cream of the worlds athletes will be there. I'll enter you in the Decathlon and Pentathlon and you'll come back famous. Famous enough to sell out the entire football season and command any amount of money you want in pro ball later.

JIM THORPE

But I want it now.

POP WARNER

All good things come to those who wait. I'll make sure you continue to have some walking around money Jim. Just think it over. You've got the whole season to get ready. It's just another track meet.

JIM THORPE

Are those Olympic medals real gold?

POP WARNER

Solid gold. Twenty four carat.

JIM THORPE

Some gold might come in handy later...Let me think about it.

POP WARNER

Good! I've already leaked to the press that you're as good as on the team. Now there's just the tryouts.

JIM THORPE

White man speak with forked tongue.

POP WARNER

Jim, I've coached a thousand kids and I'll tell you what.. You can't put in what the good Lord left out.. Whatever that special ingredient is, you've got it.. in spades. This is your time...to show the world just what a scrappy little half breed kid from Oklahoma can do. Don't let it slip away over some girl or a few pints of whiskey.

JIM THORPE

Well, since you put it like that, how could I say no?

POP WARNER

You can't Jim. You just can't.

DISSOLVE TO:

EXT. DECK OF FINLAND MORNING

Still drowsing in his deck chair, Thorpe opens one eye as Lieutenant Patton sprints past and then stops nearby to lift some barbells. Sweating profusely he is pushing himself hard.

THORPE

Morning Captain!

Patton, focusing on his workout does not acknowledge Thorpe's greeting. After several minutes Thorpe gets up, stretches, then ambles over and leans against the ships railing, observing Patton.

THORPE (CONT'D)

I'll tell you something.. You stick with it. Keep lifting those weights and trying your hardest.. and one of these days... you'll be as strong as I was... when I was ten.

Laughter erupts from anyone within earshot except for Patton, who drops the weights to the deck, his face crimson from exertion and rage. As he turns towards Thorpe, his fists clenched and murder in his eyes, a thin, wraithlike man in European clothing, inserts himself between the two men with the grace of a matador. Sporting a monocle and his face a gruesome mosaic of dueling scars, he places his hand on Patton's chest.

COUNT VOLKSMAR

(softly but firmly) Lieutenant!! Control yourself. Now is not the time.

Gradually, the words take effect and Patton relaxes, his eyes locked with Thorpe's as Volksmar leads him away. Thorpe is immediately surrounded by other Olympic team members, including Avery Brundadge.

AVERY BRUNDADGE

(sternly) You better watch yourself Thorpe.

THORPE

Friend of yours Avery?

AVERY BRUNDADGE

Not before today he wasn't.

THORPE

You two make a cute couple. Don't forget to invite me to the wedding.

### AVERY BRUNDADGE

You think you're just the cats pajama's don't you? Well your time is coming my friend. Mark my words.

### THORPE

Just when would that be Tarzan? Probably way past your bedtime. Now run along, before me and the boys decide to lower your ears a little.

Avery moves on, eventually catching up to Patton and Volksmar. EXT. UPPER DECK OF THE FINLAND – MORNING

### HARRY

(Voiceover) Well things generally settled down around the ship after that and we got down to the business at hand, which was gettin ready to lick the rest of the world at the Olympics. Howard the nigra, who everybody says is the fastest man on earth white or colored, tole me the Olympics was going to take the place of bloody war.

### HARRY (CONT'D)

Instead of everybody chopp'in and shoot'in each other up and having a heap of funerals and hard feelings, all the Czars and Kings and Presidents had a meeting and put their heads together and decided they would do like ancient Zeus and Mercury and that bunch and every four years, have a contest to see who would have bragging rights until the next one. I asked Howard what was they going to do with all the cannons and rifles and swords and such and he said they would just have to knock em into plowshares and the whole business was of biblical portions. After he tole me that, I got kind of solemn and religious, being the team mascot and everything, so I reckoned I would go to church the next morning but at the last minute I back slid and went up on deck to have a smoke.

EXT. UPPER DECK OF THE FINLAND SUNDAY MORNING

Harry and Pluck arrive on deck to find it empty except for members of the ships crew. One solitary figure stands at the rail. The intermittent sound of spirited hymnal singing comes and goes with the breeze.

### ABEL KIVIAT

Good morning Harry! How goes the mascot business?

### HARRY

Morn'in Abel. Pretty good I guess. It's a new trade for me. There's a lot to learn.

### ABEL KIVIAT

(laughing) You're a bright lad. You'll have the knack of it in no time.

### HARRY

I sure hope so. I don't want to let Colonel Thompson and the rest of the team down....Just what is a mascot supposed to do anyway Abel?

ABEL KIVIAT

Well...some people believe that a mascot has supernatural or magical powers. Powers that can influence the outcome of certain events.

HARRY

I sure don't feel very magical. But I'll give it my best shot when the time comes.

ABEL KIVIAT

You'll do just fine Harry.

HARRY

How come you to not be in church Abel?

ABEL KIVIAT

I'm Jewish Harry. Our Sabbath is from sunset on Friday until three stars appear in the evening sky on Saturday.

HARRY

Jewish? Is that the same as being a Jew?

ABEL KIVIAT

(laughing) Yes.

HARRY

That's right. The Colonel said you was a Jew.. You don't look like any Jew I ever seen. Not at all.

ABEL KIVIAT

Do you have different churches in Toledo Harry?

HARRY

Sure! We got Baptists and Methodists and Presbyterians and Catholics. Bunches of em.

ABEL KIVIAT

What about Alma? He's Mormon. Does he look any different to you?

HARRY

Alma? No. Is a Mormon a Jew?

ABEL KIVIAT

No. He's Christian. They are all Christians. And just like Christians, we Jews have sects. Different groups of people within the faith who choose to worship God in their own way. Just because I don't have a beard or wear a long black coat... It doesn't make me any less of a Jew.... Why aren't you in church this morning?

HARRY

Sometimes I just don't feel all that churchy... Mostly on Sundays.

ABEL KIVIAT

(laughing) Me too Harry. Especially on Sundays. Well I better get on with my training. It's one of the few benefits of being a Jew.

HARRY

What's that Abel?

ABEL KIVIAT

Look around! I pretty much have the whole ship to myself. I might get some dirty looks, but I think it's worth it.

HARRY

What do you do if somebody says somethin?

ABEL KIVIAT

(crossing his eyes) I cross my eyes...and ask them to try and see things my way.

HARRY

(laughing) That's a good'un Abel. Mind if I use it?

ABEL KIVIAT

Be my guest. And good luck with the mascot training.

HARRY

Thanks. See you at supper.

Abel gives a casual salute and jogs away.
EXT. DECK OF FINLAND – NIGHT

Harry is leaning on the ships railing. Lieutenant Patton strolls by with his wife and friends. Spotting Harry, Patton excuses himself and approaches.

LIEUTENANT PATTON

Ahoy there sailor!

HARRY

(saluting) Evening Sir!

LIEUTENANT PATTON

(looking Harry over) At ease. Quite the shiner you've got there. Did you put a steak on it?

HARRY

No sir. If I'd a had a steak I would have cooked it.

LIEUTENANT PATTON

(laughing) Right you are lad. I might have done the same myself, or fed it to your pup. Fine looking animal.. Unusual breed. What of its temperament?

HARRY

Oh, she don't have a temper really. She's just a peach. And smart as a whip.

LIEUTENANT PATTON

(shaking his head and smiling) Where are you berthed?

HARRY

Down in steerage. It's just grand! And mostly good company, what with the coloreds and all.

LIEUTENANT PATTON

(showing his displeasure) We can't have that... Team mates or not, it sets a bad precedent. I'll have a word with the Captain and make some other arrangements for you.

HARRY

Oh, no sir! Please don't! I'd feel a whole lot better if we just kept the President out of the whole affair. I'm fine, really I am.

LIEUTENANT PATTON

Oil and water Harry. One cannot mix the races. It is Gods will... And now, with Jim Crow, the law of the land that coloreds and whites be kept separate.

HARRY

(resignedly) I don't want to be breakin' no laws! It's just that .. I know we're bettern they are and everything...But for the life of me, I can't seem to put a finger on HOW is all... Oh! I haven't thanked you for gettin that sailor off of me yesterday.

LIEUTENANT PATTON

Think nothing of it. I just can't stomach a bully, of any sort.

HARRY

How'd you manage to tangle him up like that? He's way bigger than you!

LIEUTENANT PATTON

A little ju-jitsu goes a long way Harry.

HARRY

Jew get what?

LIEUTENANT PATTON

Ju-jitsu. An Oriental discipline of unarmed combat I studied at West Point. Size doesn't matter. In fact, your opponents size can be used against them.

HARRY

I sure could use some of that. Seems like everybody is bigger than me.

LIEUTENANT PATTON

The good book says "Pride goeth before a fall". And, it has been my experience, that the bigger they are the harder they fall. You'll come into your own Harry. All in good time.

Lieutenant Patton and Harry stand at the railing, silent for a moment gazing at the star filled sky.

HARRY

How many stars do you reckon there are sir?

LIEUTENANT PATTON

There's no counting them Harry. The good Lord in his infinite wisdom, placed them in the heavens to forever remind us of our inconsequence in the scheme of things....Can you find the Big Dipper?

HARRY

Sure, anybody can. (pointing) It's right there.

LIEUTENANT PATTON

Well done. Now... draw an imaginary line from the leading edge of the cup...bottom to top and extend it until you find a faint star just down and to the right... Do you see it?

HARRY

Sure... That's not much of a star. What of it?

LIEUTENANT PATTON

It is the North Star. The one star in all the heavens that does not move. Since the beginning of time men have relied on it as a guide. To keep them on course and bring them home safe. Some men are like that Harry, not the brightest or the biggest... but the most constant.. unwavering.. and true.

HARRY

Are you like that sir? Steady?

LIEUTENANT PATTON

It is my aspiration...May God find me worthy...Well, good night. Keep a sharp lookout for icebergs...and bodies.

HARRY

Really sir? From the Titanic? It's been over two months now. Gravely, Patton nods yes.

HARRY (CONT'D)

Would we stop to fish em out?

LIEUTENANT PATTON

Of course. We must honor the dead. And the body as vessel of the divine... Returning a daughter or father to the family and the solace it brings is truly inestimable...I believe we live many lives Harry. Each one precious...

HARRY

I've heard tell of that! Re-in-tar-nation.

LIEUTENANT PATTON

(laughing) ReinCARnation Harry. From the Latin, to have more than one body. But I'm afraid it's much too late to explore that particular subject. Our day of rest is over and the morning comes soon enough... Good night sailor.

HARRY

(saluting) Night sir.

EXT. DECK OF FINLAND DAY – MORNING
HARRY

(VO) Well Sunday was kind of restful and uneventful, the highlight bein' first mate Chatfield showing me his dancin' Hula girl tattoo. Seems we was all kinda homesick and lonesome so all the fellers hit the hay pretty early, but come Monday mornin' it was business as usual.

Lieutenant Patton and several members of the fencing team are observing a lively match. The smaller duellist quickly gains advantage and disarms its opponent to the applause of the onlookers.

LIEUTENANT PATTON

(whispering to Volkmar) Not too shabby.

COUNT VOLKMAR

Did you notice the shift to the left foot just before the final parry?

LIEUTENANT PATTON

No

COUNT VOLKMAR

Watch for it. It adds several centimeters to the lunge.

(applauding) Well done! Excellent! Would you accept a challenge from my protege?

Without removing the protective fencing gear the winner nods their approval and assumes a defensive position. Patton steps into the competition lane.

LIEUTENANT PATTON

En Garde!!

Blades flash with no obvious advantage to either combatant and no points scored. Finally Patton, anticipating the unorthodox shift to the front foot feints to the side and avoids the thrust.

Countering with a perfectly timed offensive move, he delivers a lethal touch and his opponent concedes defeat.

LIEUTENANT PATTON (CONT'D)

I really thought you had me there. Why haven't I come up against you before Sir?

Sword tip on the ground, his opponent removes the protective head gear revealing a mass of golden curls that fall to the back of her knees. Patton is opened mouthed but Volkmar is grinning, his facial scars enhancing his pleasure in the ruse.

VIOLET MACY

(angrily, eyes flashing) Keep your sir's to yourself. Perhaps now you will not be so quick to dismiss women from their rightful place in these Olympic games.

COUNT VOLKMAR

Permit me to introduce you Herr Patton, to Miss Violet Macy. Her father was a schoolmate of mine at University in Berlin.

Introductions are made with Patton bowing formally. Violet continues staring at Patton.

LIEUTENANT PATTON

Schoolmates you say. Does he carry the same marks of honor as yourself?
(gesturing to the multiple dueling scars on Volkmars face)

COUNT VOLKMAR

Fewer, certainly, but with no loss of honor. He was my superior in all things. Fathering willful daughters but one of his many accomplishments.

VIOLET MACY

So, Lieutenant. Why are you so adamantly against equality for women.

LIEUTENANT PATTON

Miss Macy, I have never held the opinion that the sexes are equal. On the contrary. My Mother and dear sister saw to it, from an early age, that I was well schooled in the deficiencies of the male. That is why we are forever confined to the menial tasks of labor and defending the hearth, leaving the far more lofty pursuits of civilization and child rearing to those who hold some promise of success.

VIOLET MACY

Don't waste your homespun philosophies on me Lieutenant. I am well aware of your opposition to the Suffragettes and your desire to continue the enslavement of women and...

COUNT VOLKMAR

(interrupting) Perhaps a change of topic is called for. Let us continue our training and resume this political discussion at a later time. Shall we?

VIOLET MACY

Of course Count. You are right as always. I am rather behind this morning, in my pursuit of civilization.

Laughs all around. Patton notices Harry standing to the side and waves him over.

LIEUTENANT PATTON

Harry!.. Let me introduce you to Miss Macy. Miss Macy, this is Harry Naughton, mascot and good luck charm of the team.

Harry sidles over smoking a homemade cigarette, somewhat in awe of this Amazonian fencer.

HARRY

(bowing awkwardly) Pleased to meet you Maam!

VIOLET MACY

Well I am not pleased to see you smoking that disgusting cigarette!

HARRY

(red faced) Sorry Ma'am... I'll save it for later.

Putting out the cigarette on the bottom of his shoe, Harry places the butt in his jacket pocket.

VIOLET MACY

(exasperated) You would do well to throw those nasty things in the sea! A fine young man such as yourself wasting his health and looks. For what? So that you stink and your teeth yellow. Coffin nails. That's all they are. Gott in Himmel.

Patton and the others laugh as Harry is decimated by Violet.

HARRY

Sorry Miss Violet. I didn't know just havin a smoke could do all those things. I sure would hate to give it up. I been smokin since I was five.

VIOLET MACY

Then you should stop this instant! Before you do yourself irreparable harm.

HARRY

You reckon if I give it up, I could learn to sword fight like you?

VIOLET MACY

If you promise to stop, I will personally give you your first lesson. Right now.

Solemnly, Harry raises his hand and crosses his heart.

HARRY

I swear...Now lets get to it!

VIOLET MACY

Your first lesson is not to swear in front of a Lady!

Laughter all around.

VIOLET MACY (CONT'D)

I will be observing you to see if you are sincere in your intentions Master Naughton. Perhaps we can continue your lessons at a later date.

Violet curtsies.

VIOLET MACY (CONT'D)

Gentlemen... Good day.

Gracefully, Violet turns and walks away. All the men watch her intently as she leaves.

HARRY

There ain't nothin' like her in Toledo Lieutenant.

LIEUTENANT PATTON

Not yet Harry, but there will be. She's already wearing the pants, God help us if they get the vote.

COUNT VOLKMAR

I must say, the pants do become her.

LIEUTENANT PATTON

That, Count, is what we call ten pounds of female in a five pound sack.

COUNT VOLKMAR

Lieutenant! And you a married man!

LIEUTENANT PATTON

Just because I'm on a diet Count, doesn't mean I can't look at the menu.

The men are transfixed by her departure until she turns out of sight.
LIEUTENANT PATTON

(coughing) Well..I must take my leave gentlemen. Mrs. Patton is expecting me.

COUNT VOLKMAR

(smiling) Of course Lieutenant. Give her my regards.

LIEUTENANT PATTON

Harry? See you at the swimtank at ten?

HARRY

Yessir!

With remarkable swiftness Lietenant Patton gathers his fencing gear and heads toward his cabin.
HARRY (CONT'D)

Looks like the Lieutenant was in a hurry don't it Count.

COUNT VOLKMAR

Indeed Harry. I believe he is.

INT. ENGINE ROOM OF THE FINLAND – DARK
Shattering the silence, a sledge hammer metronome strikes metal. Shirtless mechanics hold flickering oil lamps to illuminate the repairs.
CUT TO:

EXT. – DECK OF THE FINLAND – MIDDAY

The Finland is dead in the water for repairs. Members of the swim team are gathered around a ten by eight foot square canvas water tank on the deck, watching other swimmers train, awaiting their turn. Harry leans on the ships railing with Duke looking down at the ocean seventy feet below. The sun is shining and not a breath of wind on this midsummers day.

HARRY

How long you figure til we're under way again Duke?

DUKE

No tellin.. Whatever it takes. Those boys know their business.

HARRY

You reckon a feller could survive a fall from up here?

DUKE

Sure. I've dove from lots higher. A hundred feet or more.

HARRY

You're pullin my leg.

DUKE

As a boy, in the harbor we used to dive for coins from the top of the mainmast off the old whaling schooners. Really big ships.

DISSOLVE TO:

HAWAII-WAIMEA FALLS OAHU – AFTERNOON

Duke and a group of his friends are climbing lava cliffs that tower above a small pool. A waterfall from a pristine stream emphasizes the height. Reaching the top, each boy takes his turn diving into an impossibly small area below.

DISSOLVE TO:

EXT. DECK OF THE FINLAND – DAY
HARRY

I'd of liked to have seen that!

DUKE

You can see it right now if you want. We're not going anywhere soon and I'm last in line to use the pool, as usual... Haoles.

HARRY

What's a howlie?

DUKE

You're a haole. Any one who's white.

HARRY

Is that why you have to wait to use the pool?

DUKE

Bingo.

Already wearing his swimsuit, Duke climbs up on the railing, stretching his arms wide and flexing his muscles, clowning in preparation for the dive. Lieutenant Patton and Avery Brundage, toweling their heads dry after leaving the swim tank, join Violet Macy and a small crowd which has gathered in anticipation of the dive.

JIM THORPE

(loudly) Whoop! Whoop! Give em Duke!

LIEUTENANT PATTON

What the hell does he think he's doing? He'll break his fool neck!

JIM THORPE

Easy now Captain. Us Injuns got thick skulls AND stiff necks doncha know?

LIEUTENANT PATTON

Damn you Thorpe! This is a team effort. A United States of America team! And that's a gold medal about to sink to the bottom of the ocean.

AVERY BRUNDAGE

(dramatically) No man can survive a fall from that height! I'm putting a stop to this right now.

(shouting) Duke!! Duke!!

Duke, hearing his name, takes it as a signal to dive. Powerfully launching himself up and out, he executes a perfect Swan dive, entering the water with barely a splash. Silence prevails, all eyes riveted on the small white ring of foam that has swallowed Duke. Staying submerged for dramatic effect, he surfaces a full minute later to the cheers and applause of all on deck.

JIM THORPE

See Captain? No sweat... Your turn Avery.

CUT TO:

ENGINE ROOM OF THE FINLAND – DARK

Two sweating mechanics work in tandem, turning a colossal wrench on a six foot diameter nut. Straining with all their might until it will go no further.

SEAMAN FLYNN

By God and the Virgin, that's all she'll go.

SEAMAN TANNER

Good enough. Fire her up boys. And pour it on. The sooner we make Antwerp the sooner I'm rid of the lot of you.

SEAMAN FLYNN

Now darlin', don't be talkin' that a ways. What would you do without us?

SEAMAN TANNER

I'd hire the first bunch of drunken, lice infested circus monkeys I could find and know for a fact, that I'm two rungs higher up Jacobs ladder than where I sit right now.

Good natured laughter fills the engine room as the men return to their work.

CUT TO:

EXT. DECK OF THE FINLAND – MIDDAY

Avery scowls at Thorpe then, is abruptly jolted into him as the ships engines engage and the Finland gets underway. Making the most of his time in the water, swimming and diving for coins thrown from above, Duke is unaware of the movement of the ship. Too late, he starts to swim after the Finland. A large wave from the wake of the departing ship looms threateningly over Duke and a concerted gasp escapes the lips of all those watching.

DISSOLVE TO:

HAWAII WAIKIKI OAHU SURF BREAK – DAY

Duke and a small group of friends sit on wooden surfboards in a flat blue ocean, looking out to sea. Far out on the horizon a faint dark line appears.

SARGE KAHANAMOKU

Here they come!

Immediately, all the boys lie prone on their boards and begin to paddle furiously towards the approaching line. Looming now, a solid 15 foot wave is forming, the light offshore breeze pushing it higher and higher. Duke, the strongest paddler has reached the peak of the wave, leaving his companions strung out behind him in the impact zone. As his fellows stand on their boards and dive off hoping to get as deep as possible before the lip of the wave lands on their heads, Duke paddles up the face of the monster wave. Sitting back on his board, he lifts the nose out of the water and spins, pointing the board towards the beach. Paddling hard, the board starts to move with the wave and Duke catches it, jumping gracefully to his feet as a thick lip of seawater pitches out behind him. Free falling now, he manages to bury the rail of his board into the face of the wave and dragging his foot in the water steers it past the loose boards of his companions. Sliding and carving toward the beach, Duke smiles broadly as a chorus of joyful hoots mingle with the crashing surf.

DISSOLVE TO:

EXT. DECK OF THE FINLAND – MIDDAY
                     HARRY

Swim Duke! Swim.

Swimming powerfully, Duke pulls in front of the wake and pushing out his chest, bodysurfs the trailing wave. Appreciative applause and cheers from the ship encourage him to show off and he spins several times before losing the wave. Lieutenant Patton is the first onboard to realize Dukes predicament. Grabbing a lifesaving ring labeled FINLAND he turns to Harry.
                 LIEUTENANT PATTON

He can't make it Harry!!.. He'll be left behind!.. Go straight to the Captain and have him bring the ship about.

              LIEUTENANT PATTON (CONT'D)

Tell him "man over board" Go now!!

Lieutenant Patton heaves the life ring over the railing as Harry weaves through the athletes and passengers on deck making his way to the bridge.
INT. BRIDGE OF THE FINLAND DAY
Bursting into the bridge he finds the Captain and Colonel Thompson, teacups and saucers in hand.
                     HARRY

(breathless) Man overboard! Man overboard!

                 COLONEL THOMPSON

What's this now? Get your wits about you Harry! Who's overboard?

HARRY

Duke sir, He jumped off the ship!

COLONEL THOMPSON

Duke? The Hawaiian? Why on earth would he jump ship?

HARRY

There's no time sir! We've got to turn around and get him!

CAPTAIN THOMAS

Turn around? Out of the question. When did this happen lad?

HARRY

When the ship was stopped. He..He dove off the railing.

COLONEL THOMPSON

Was he injured? Is he conscious?

HARRY

He tried to swim and catch the ship, but it was too fast for him. Please sir, it was Lieutenant Patton tole me to come. We just gotta save him!

COLONEL THOMPSON

Lieutenant Patton eh? Well Captain... Man overboard!

CAPTAIN THOMAS

(grumbling) All engines full stop.

FIRST MATE

Aye aye Captain, All engines stop.

CAPTAIN THOMAS

Colonel? Would you be so kind as to inquire into our man overboard and relay any further information to the bridge?

COLONEL THOMPSON

My pleasure Captain. Come along Harry and we'll see what can be done.

EXT. DECK OF THE FINLAND – DAY

Harry and the Colonel hurry back to the ships railing where a large crowd has gathered.

HARRY

Where is he? Can you see him?

JIM THORPE

See that little black dot. That's him.

COLONEL THOMPSON

Good God Allmighty!... Harry! Run and tell the Captain to bring the ship about. It's life or death! Go like the wind!

Harry takes off back towards the bridge.
JIM THORPE

We can put him in the meat locker to warm him up once he's back aboard Colonel.

COLONEL THOMPSON

This is no joke Thorpe. What in the name of God possessed the man to jump?

LIEUTENANT PATTON

I would have to guess boredom sir. And he didn't jump, he dove... A perfect swan dive.

COLONEL THOMPSON

Headfirst? He could easily have been injured.. or killed.. He might still succumb to hypothermia.

LIEUTENANT PATTON

It was sublime.

COLONEL THOMPSON

Come again?

LIEUTENANT PATTON

It was the most beautiful thing I have ever seen in the field of athletics.

VIOLET MACY

For once I agree with you Lieutenant. Truly...Sublime.

With stars in her eyes, Violet moves away to aid the rescue.

COLONEL THOMPSON

(wistfully) Bully! I wish I could have seen it... Well, fish him out and pray he's not the worse for wear.

JIM THORPE

I'd a jumped in after him Colonel, but I didn't want to break training.

COLONEL THOMPSON

Do you know what my dear old Grandmother used to tell me Thorpe?

JIM THORPE

Five to one I'm gonna find out.

COLONEL THOMPSON

She said, Robert my dear...Nobody likes a smart ass.

JIM THORPE

Yes sir. Sorry sir.

COLONEL THOMPSON

Carry on.

Shivering, Duke is brought on board and wrapped in blankets by Violet who takes charge of his recovery.

COLONEL THOMPSON (CONT'D)

Duke

DUKE

(stammering) Yy yees ss SSir.

COLONEL THOMPSON

That was a damn fool thing you did son. This team needs all its members whole and healthy if we are to triumph at the games.

DUKE

Ss sorrry Ss sir.

COLONEL THOMPSON

Lets keep the swimming in the training tank from now on shall we?

DUKE

YYeess ssirr.

COLONEL THOMPSON

No harm done... Miss Macy?

VIOLET MACY

Yes Colonel?

COLONEL THOMPSON

Will you see to it that Duke gets below? And get some hot soup in him.

VIOLET MACY

(vigorously rubbing Dukes shoulders) Of course. It will be my pleasure.

COLONEL THOMPSON

Very well then. I shall leave you in Miss Macys good hands. We reach Antwerp tomorrow and there are plans for an exhibition.. Duke, one more thing.

DUKE

Ssirr?

COLONEL THOMPSON

The next time you dive... make sure I'm in attendance... Do we have a deal?

DUKE

(shivering violently) Dddeeal...CCoorrnnel.

INT. DINING HALL FINLAND – NIGHT

The dining hall has been cleared of tables and chairs. An orchestra plays a slow waltz. The Captain of the Finland stands with Colonel Thompson, Count Volkmar, Pop Warner and several other well dressed passengers on the sidelines, observing the dancers. Lieutenant Patton in full military dress, is commanding the dance floor with his wife.

COLONEL THOMPSON

What a fine couple they make! Four thousand years of civilization in full flower before our eyes.

POP WARNER

I concur Colonel. Seems like only yesterday I was swinging from a tree by my tail, my only worry where the next banana was coming from.

COUNT VOLKMAR

For many of you Colonials, Mr. Warner, I'm afraid it was but yesterday.

POP WARNER

Now hold on just a minute there Count! I resemble that remark!

Good natured laughter from the group.
CAPTAIN THOMAS

Hardly, Mr. Warner.. Unfortunately, some of your charges do.

A moment of awkward silence is relieved by the spirited arrival of several members of the Olympic team led by Jim Thorpe. Colonel Thompson moves to welcome them.
COLONEL THOMPSON

Gentlemen! Glad you decided to come this evening!

JIM THORPE

Wild horses couldn't keep me away Colonel! I've been itchin' to kick up my heels a little.

The Waltz has ended and Lieutenant Patton and his wife exit the dance floor, joining the group of onlookers

Miss Violet Macy has just arrived, accompanied by her father, Baron Macy.

### COUNT VOLKMAR

Lieutenant, allow me to introduce Baron Macy. And of course you know his lovely daughter Violet.

### LIEUTENANT PATTON

(shaking hands) Sir. An honor. I had the privilege of making your daughters acquaintance earlier today Baron. A surprise attack I'm afraid.

### BARON MACY

So I heard Lieutenant. It is rare to meet a survivor of my daughters charms.

### COUNT VOLKMAR

Baron, may I present Mrs. Patton.. And Mr. Warner.

### BARON MACY

Charmed...Mr. Warner..Are you the mentor of that remarkable Indian fellow? What is his name?

### POP WARNER

Thorpe. Jim Thorpe.

### BARON MACY

Yes! That's it. They say these Aboriginals...

### VIOLET MACY

(embarrassed) Father, Please! Do not bore us with your antiquated theories.

### BARON MACY

Forgive me. My daughter is correct. I am a bore. Let us enjoy the music shall we? Perhaps you would honor Violet with a dance Lieutenant? With your permission of course Mrs. Patton.

### MRS. PATTON

Of course.. if the Baron will accompany me to the punch bowl.

### BARON MACY

(bowing deeply) At your service Madame.

A waltz has been playing for quite a while as Patton and Violet move onto the dance floor. Patton is a competent but somewhat stiff dancer, keeping Violet at arms length and avoiding eye contact until the end of the waltz. As the music ends they separate and applaud demurely. Suddenly beside them, Jim Thorpe appears.

### JIM THORPE

Mind if I cut in Captain?

### LIEUTENANT PATTON

(stunned) Yes! I do! This is completely unacceptable!

VIOLET MACY

Not to me! I accept. Thank you for the dance Lieutenant. Give my regards to Mrs. Patton.

JIM THORPE

Swell! Names Jim. What's yours? (saluting) Captain.

Taking her arm, Thorpe whisks Violet away and Patton is left standing alone on the dance floor, red faced and enraged.

VIOLET MACY

You may call me Violet.

JIM THORPE

Violet. That's real pretty. Now, listen Violet, I slipped the band leader a little something to try and lively up the party a little.

VIOLET MACY

Wonderful!

Thorpe, with forefinger touching thumb gives the OK to the band leader who returns an exaggerated wink.

As the uptempo notes of a fiery Tango emanate from the orchestra, Thorpe and Violet whirl away, leaving Patton standing on the dance floor. Patton returns to the sidelines and joins his wife as Violet and Thorpe put on an amazing dance performance. People are frowning and clucking their tongues, but the grace and beauty of the young dancers is truly a wonder. As the song comes to a spirited end, the Baron, Pop Warner and the Patton's stand with a large group, applauding.

POP WARNER

Well I'll be a monkeys Uncle! That's one of my Aboriginals for you...Collegiate ballroom dancing champion, 1912.

CUT TO:

EXT. DECK OF FINLAND – NIGHT

Duke, barefoot and dressed in his Olympic uniform sits with Harry on deck. Under the stars, Duke plays his ukulele and sings.

DUKE

Aloha Oye..Aloha Oye..

Duke finishes the song and listens for a moment to the ships engines as Harry lights up a smoke.

HARRY

How come you decided not to go to the dance Duke?

DUKE

Sometimes the idea of going is better than going.

HARRY

I don't follow you.

DUKE

Well, I got all dressed up and was ready to go. But once I was there and started to go inside, I saw all those rich people, and the way they look at me...like I had escaped from the zoo or something. I just figured It would be more comfortable for everyone if I stayed outside.

HARRY

Anywhere's is more comfortable if'n you can take your shoes off for a spell.

Both Harry and Duke laugh, leaning back and wiggling their toes. Taking some air on the deck after the dance, Colonel Thompson and a group approach.

COLONEL THOMPSON

Well boys, how are you this fine evening?

Both Harry and Duke jump up to greet the Colonel.

HARRY

Just dandy Colonel!

DUKE

Fine Colonel.

COLONEL THOMPSON

All thawed out after your swim this morning Duke?

DUKE

(sheepishly) Yes sir. Sorry to be a bother.

COLONEL THOMPSON

Nonsense! It's to be expected. All this pent up energy. It's a wonder the whole team didn't follow you in. What's that you've got there?

DUKE

This? This is my ukulele.

COLONEL THOMPSON

I've never seen anything like it. Some sort of a miniature guitar?

DUKE

Kind of. My father gave it to me so that if I got homesick, I could play and be right back on the beach.

COLONEL THOMPSON

Well does it work? Can you transport us all to the Islands...right now?

Laughter and murmurs of encouragement from the Colonels group.

DUKE

Oh, I don't know..

HARRY

Sure Duke! You can do it! Just play that last one you was playin. Old o ha oil. It was awful sweet.

COLONEL THOMPSON

What do you say Duke?

DUKE

All right. Here goes.

Duke sits down and strums and sings Aloha Oye. As he finishes, there is not a dry eye among the women in the group.

COLONEL THOMPSON

Splendid! Just grand! You know Duke, I have been to the South Seas and I swear, your father was right. I felt as if I was truly there as you played. Thank you.

MRS. PATTON

Aloha? What does it mean?

DUKE

It means many things. Love. Hello, good bye. A wish that all is well with you and yours.

MRS. PATTON

One word can mean all that? Extraordinary. It was beautiful Duke. How does one say thank you in your native tongue?

DUKE

Mahalo. That's the Hawaiian way to say thanks.

MRS. PATTON

Well then many Mahalo's and Aloha for now... George? We must sail there one day. Promise me.

LIEUTENANT PATTON

One day. I promise. Let's get these Olympics out of the way and then see if the Kaiser can keep his shirt on a little longer. What do you say Baron?

BARON MACY

I don't have my crystal ball with me this evening Lieutenant. But I will say, that politics are best left until after breakfast.

COLONEL THOMPSON

Well said Baron. Thank you all for a memorable evening.. You boys should hit the hay. We reach Antwerp tomorrow and you'll have to find your land legs.. Good night everyone.

The group moves on toward their respective cabins leaving Harry and Duke alone on deck.

HARRY

Where do you reckon our land legs might be hid at?

DUKE

(laughing) Is this your first time on a ship?

HARRY

Yep.

DUKE

You get used to the rolling of the deck and then when you disembark, you can't hardly stand. I fell right down when we came into San Francisco. Takes a little while before you can walk straight.

HARRY

You funnin' me Duke?

DUKE

You'll find out tomorrow.

HARRY

I'll wager I don't fall down.

DUKE

I'd take that bet if I had anything worth betting.

HARRY

We could swap pocket knives... If I fall down gettin' off the ship tomorrow, I get your knife and you can have mine.

Harry spits in his palm and offers it to Duke.
DUKE

You're on.

Duke spits in his palm and the two shake hands.
EXT. DOCKSIDE ANTWERP BELGIUM – MORNING
Longshoremen secure the Finland and the gangplank is let down. Eager passengers and athletes disembark, many having difficulty walking as they set foot on the dock. Duke has come ahead of Harry anticipating his arrival.
HARRY

(waving) Hey Duke! Wait for me!!

Harry and Pluck hurry down the gangplank, both of them weaving drunkenly as their feet hit the dock. First Harry, then his struggling pup fall. Several more seasoned travelers laugh good-naturedly at their plight. Duke moves forward and gives Harry a hand up.

DUKE

What did I tell you?

HARRY

(bewildered) Don't that beat all!. Well here's your knife.

DUKE

I don't want your old knife. It was a suckers bet. I knew what was going to happen.. C'mon I told the Colonel I'd meet him at the Natatorium.

HARRY

The Nate a whatium?

DUKE

(laughing ) The swimming pool. C'mon we're late.

EXT. ANTWERP STADIUM – DAY

The stadium is full of spectators. Flags and banners flutter in a warm breeze. Various track and field events are underway as the running high jump begins. The bar is set at six feet.

THORPE

My grandma could clear six feet carryin' two chickens and a haunch of venison.

AVERY BRUNDAGE

Stolen from some poor farmers smokehouse I'll bet.

THORPE

Maybe... Times WAS tough after Wounded Knee... Give it a go there wannabe.. I mean Avery.

Avery runs at the bar, barely clears it and lands HARD in the sand pit. Alma Richards, George Horine and Jim Thorpe follow, clearing the bar easily.

THORPE (CONT'D)

(shouting) Hey Pop! Take it up a couple inches. Lets get this over with.

POP WARNER

Don't forget who's the coach here Jim... I'll go six one and a half.

Alma easily clears the bar followed by Horine and Thorpe. Avery misses on two consecutive attempts and is out of the competition.

THORPE

(In mock announcers voice) Tough luck for the young cowboy folks. He'll be back, just bruised his pride is all.

POP WARNER

OK, six feet two inches. Lets see what you've got.

Thorpe, Richards and Horine easily clear the bar.

POP WARNER (CONT'D)

This could go on all day boys. What's your record George?
Six five and a half?

GEORGE HORINE

World record Coach. The whole wide world.

POP WARNER

Well, what do you say Alma?

Alma is not looking good with a bad eye infection. He wears a
floppy hat to cut the glare of midday sun.

ALMA RICHARDS

The Lord is my strength. His will be done.

POP WARNER

All right then, it's you boys and King Richards the Crusader
going for six foot five inches... Alma!

ALMA RICHARDS

Yes coach?

POP WARNER

Have the doc take a look at that eye. It's just nasty.

ALMA RICHARDS

Sure thing Coach.

Alma attempts his first jump and slips on the approach, missing badly. Trying again he knocks the bar off with his foot and is out of the competition.

POP WARNER

Jim? I don't think you've gone six five before.

THORPE
Not until today Coach.

Thorpe makes his approach and nearly clears but his leg grazes the bar and wobbling, it falls to the ground.

POP WARNER

George? Ready?

George Horine, makes his approach and leaps, knocking the bar down with his heel.

POP WARNER (CONT'D)

Jim? Last try at this height. Avery says you should consider leaving the chickens behind.

THORPE

OK white bread. Watch this.

DISSOLVE TO:

INT. POOL HALL – NIGHT

Jim Thorpe is shooting pool with friends and classmates. Most are wearing sweaters emblazoned with the big "C" of the Carlise Indian school. Beers in hand they are celebrating.

ALBERT EXIDINE

It's your shot Grampa.

Thorpe walks around the table setting up his shot.
JIM THORPE

You boys might just as well sit down while I run the table.

Jim makes his first two shots then scratches the cue ball after shooting too hard.
LEWIS TEWANIMA

(moving to take his turn) YOU sit down Jim. Your going to need all your strength for the Olympics.

ALBERT EXIDINE

He can rest on the ship. Pop Warner says there's a deck chair with his name on it already.

JIM THORPE

I'm not taking the ship. I'm gonna jump to Sweden!

Standing flat footed, Jim crouches low then jumps up and sideways across the pool table, landing like a cat on the opposite side. A moment of shocked silence then hoots of praise fill the pool hall.
JIM THORPE (CONT'D)

(laughing) With these legs, I could jump to the moon!

Cheers and war whoops fill the pool hall.
DISSOLVE TO:
EXT. ANTWERP STADIUM – DAY
The cheers of the pool hall change to the cheers of the stadium. Thorpe looks around then directly at Avery. Giving a bloodcurdling

war whoop he runs in a circle then full speed at the bar. Seeming to fly, he easily clears the height and lands softly in the sand pit.

POP WARNER

Thank you VERY much Avery. George? Last try. Give it all you've got.

George takes a few breaths then makes his approach. He goes up effortlessly then twists, clearing the bar with all but his toe which hits the bar, knocking it to the ground. Stunned, he congratulates Thorpe.

GEORGE HORINE

Nice job old man. Didn't think you had it in you.

THORPE

Thanks Champ.

GEORGE HORINE

Can I get another try Pops?

POP WARNER

Sure, but it won't count for the meet. You're only allowed the two attempts.

GEORGE HORINE

Just for my pride then.

POP WARNER

All right, give it a go.

George focuses on the bar then begins a slow approach, gradually picking up speed then fluidly launching himself over the bar, easily clearing the height.

POP WARNER (CONT'D)

Bravo! Keep that in your pocket for Stockholm George. Jim? You're allowed to keep going if you want. It won't go on the record books as this isn't a sanctioned meet, but you're welcome to try.

THORPE

Let's call it macaroni for today Coach. It's way past my beer time any ways.

POP WARNER

When is it NOT your beer time? All right, you boys have earned it. Hit the showers and I'll see you aboard ship. Remember it's lights out at ten sharp.

THORPE

Ten o'clock in New York, or Antwerp?

POP WARNER

I'm not going to dignify that with a reply Thorpe. Just try and keep your nose clean. Now beat it.

EXT. STOCKHOLM SWEDEN OLYMPIC STADIUM – DAY

Opening ceremonies. Athletes from all nations parade. Harry and Pluck march with the United States team with Harry carrying the 46 star American flag.

CUT TO:

EXT. STOCKHOLM STADIUM – MIDDAY

In running shorts and sweat soaked t-shirt Lieutenant Patton enters the filled to capacity stadium weaving and stumbling. With blurred vision he sees the finish line and hears the cheers of the crowd as from a distance, his own labored panting and the rapid beating of his heart drowning out all other sounds. Closing his eyes he hears the extremely loud report of a 38 caliber pistol held at arms length, the gun sight in sharp focus and pointed precisely at the slightly out of focus bulls eye of a circular target.

DISSOLVE TO:

EXT. OLYMPIC PISTOL RANGE STOCKHOLM – DAY
CAPTAIN FRANK MCCOY

(lowering a pair of binoculars) By God, that's the stuff. You can rest easy now George. Even better than yesterday. Outstanding.

The two men wait under the shade of a nearby tree as the target is examined by the judges. Time passes as more and more officials are grouped around the target. Eventually they approach Lieutenant Patton and Captain McCoy.

OLYMPIC REFEREE

I'm afraid I have some disheartening news for you Lieutenant.

CAPTAIN FRANK MCCOY

Come again?

OLYMPIC REFEREE

It appears that two of the ten shots have missed the target.

## CAPTAIN FRANK MCCOY

(shouting) Missed?...Missed the target? Impossible. Preposterous! I spotted every shot with my binoculars. There was no miss sir.

## OLYMPIC REFEREE #2

(holding the target) As you can see, the center of the target is completely shot through. Eight perforations are clearly visible but we cannot account for the other two. I am sorry but the decision is final.

## CAPTAIN FRANK MCCOY

Like hell it is! Those bullets must have passed through the same holes. For Chrissake, the man set the course record yesterday.

## OLYMPIC REFEREE

We are aware of that Captain. If the Lieutenant had perhaps used a smaller caliber pistol, similar to the other contestants...I am sorry the decision is final.

DISSOLVE TO:

EXT. STOCKHOLM STADIUM – MIDDAY

Opening his eyes, Lieutenant Patton is no closer to the shimmering finish line. Each step is agony, the ground at his feet seeming to pull him down. Once again he closes his eyes for a moment.

DISSOLVE TO:

INT. – OLYMPIC FENCING COMPETITION – NIGHT

Two expert fencers are competing savagely, neither one seeming to have the advantage. Count Volkmar, Colonel Thompson and Harry are on the sidelines.

### COLONEL THOMPSON

The Frenchman is certainly living up to his reputation.

### COUNT VOLKMAR

He has both size and great speed. A formidable combination.

### HARRY

Lieutenant Patton tole me that size don't matter. It's like David and the Goliath, just a spoonful of Jujitsu at the right time is all it takes.

### COUNT VOLKMAR

(exclaiming) Of course! Why didn't I see it before! Harry, what a Godsend you are!

The first round of the match has ended in a draw with the competitors retiring to the sidelines. Lieutenant Patton removes his headgear to converse with Count Volkmar.

### LIEUTENANT PATTON

He's so strong! It's all I can do to stand my ground.

### COUNT VOLKMAR

Let him have it.

### LIEUTENANT PATTON

I'm doing my damnndest to let him have it.

COUNT VOLKMAR

No Lieutenant, your ground. Invite him in..THEN, when his speed and mass have pushed through the door, step aside and gently close it.

LIEUTENANT PATTON

I'm not following you Count.

COUNT VOLKMAR

Do you remember your first encounter with Miss Macy?

LIEUTENANT PATTON

Of course. Hard to forget that one.

COUNT VOLKMAR

Your opponent employs the same tactic. His great size will not allow him to withdraw after commitment. Invite him in Lieutenant, then, the coup de gras.

An official is signaling to reconvene the match as Lieutenant Patton stands and nods, replacing his headgear he heads back to the competition floor. Once again the blades flash and then the announcers voice calls

ANNOUNCER

Match to the United States..

DISSOLVE TO:

STOCKHOLM STADIUM -MIDDAY

Utterly spent now, his legs crossed up, Patton is falling. The stadium spins round, then disappears as his cheek slams into the cinder track.

DISSOLVE TO:

EXT. STEEPLE CHASE COMPETITION STOCKHOLM – DAY

Looking past the neck and head of his mount as they approach a six foot high hedge, Lieutenant Patton savagely jams his spurs into the flanks of his horse.

PATTON

You sumbitch! Don't quit on me now!

His riding crop a blur, he whoops as the horse leaps up, up and over the barrier. Landing well, horse and rider continue at full gallop over the rough terrain.

DISSOLVE TO:

EXT. STOCKHOLM SWEDEN OLYMPIC STADIUM – DAY

Various athletic events are under way as Jim Thorpe and Avery Brundage prepare to run the 200 meter high hurdles.

POP WARNER

This is it Jim. Finish in the top three now and you will have won the whole shootin' match. Decathlon and Pentathlon. Who would have guessed it?

THORPE

(gesturing with his thumb) Not Avery.

COLONEL THOMPSON

What on earth did you do to get him so riled up?

THORPE

Beat the pants off him at everything he tried that's what.

POP WARNER

I hope to God he never has the upper hand on you Jim. He's just the sort to use it.

THORPE

Not likely coach. Looks like I'll be moving in some different circles after we get back to the States.

POP WARNER

Let's hope so... Well, so as not to jinx you.. Break a leg.

THORPE

What?

POP WARNER

Just kidding.

THORPE

Thanks a lot. Now get out of here and let me bring this thing home.

Pop touches his finger to the brim of his hat and moves to the sidelines as the racers take their lanes.

OLYMPIC OFFICIAL

On your mark. Ready, steady, BANG!

The race is on and Thorpe takes an early lead. Effortlessly clearing the hurdles, he flashes back in montage to the other events he has competed in at the Olympics. Pole vaulting, discus, javelin and exhibition baseball. As he sails over the last hurdle, in the lead and approaching the finish line, the spectators in the stands let loose a deafening cheer. Assuming the accolades are for him, Jim raises his arms in victory. Noticing that no one is paying any attention to him, he glances to his left and sees Lieutenant Patton start to fall.

As Patton hits the ground, a collective gasp from the lips of ten thousand spectators is eclipsed by a deafening cheer, as a second runner enters the stadium behind him. Unconscious, Patton hears nothing. Several spectators move from the sidelines and begin to shake his shoulder and call in Swedish and English for him to get up. Slowly he opens his eyes and becomes cognizant of his surroundings. One voice cuts through the din and he manages to pull into focus the face of Jim Thorpe.

THORPE

C'mon Custer. Get up. There's girls watchin. You can sleep when you're dead.

PATTON

(mumbling) You sumbitch.

Pulling himself first to his elbows, then knees, then standing, he lurches toward the finish line to the roar of the crowd. The second place runner passes him, providing the incentive to push harder and he drunkenly makes for the finish, collapsing once again after crossing the finish line.

POP WARNER

That was mighty sporting of you Jim. I thought you two didn't get along.

JIM THORPE

We don't. I just like to make him mad.

POP WARNER

Looks like "mad" was just what the doctor ordered. Lets get moving. You've got the high jump final in ten minutes.

JIM THORPE

Are you kidding me? I'm plumb wore out. I couldn't jump a crack in the sidewalk right now.

POP WARNER

Well, you qualified for the final. You and Alma are the only Americans left.

JIM THORPE

Old Alma really turned it around didn't he?

POP WARNER

Look! There he goes now.

Alma Richards, one eye still infected and wearing his trade mark floppy hat, is preparing to jump six foot four inches. Dropping to one knee, he prays for a moment. Arising, he runs hard at the bar and easily clears the height with inches to spare.

JIM THORPE

Looks like Jesus came through in the end don't it Coach?

POP WARNER

Mysterious are the ways of the Lord.

JIM THORPE

Yup. He's as spooky as they come.

POP WARNER

It couldn't hurt for you to ask for a little help from above.

JIM THORPE

I'm still waiting for that sled I wanted for Christmas.

POP WARNER

Just get in there and jump already.

Jim checks in and attempts the jump. Missing twice, he comes in fourth, out of the medals and Alma takes the gold.
JIM THORPE

Alma! What the heck got into you?

ALMA RICHARDS

Not my will, but his be done.

JIM THORPE

(shaking hands) Well, congratulations,.. to the both of you..

ABEL KIVIAT

(shaking hands) All right Alma! Gold medal!

(checking his pocketwatch) Hey you know what? If we hurry we can see Duke swim.

JIM THORPE

I'm in. Hey guys look!

Pointing up they see a biplane flying over head.
ABEL KIVIAT

Isn't that something... They say one day you'll be able to fly across the Atlantic.

JIM THORPE

No jokin?.. You're the top flyer here today Alma. What do you think?

ALMA RICHARDS

If God had intended man to fly, he would have given him wings.

JIM THORPE

Well, He must have intended him to eat, because I could eat a horse.

ABEL KIVIAT

Amen to that. We can grab something on the way, but we better get a move on.

JIM THORPE

Lead on Moses.

INT. NATATORIUM STOCKHOLM – DAY

Crowds line the pool as competitions are underway. A trumpet blast announces the arrival of the King and Queen of Sweden who take their seats in the royal box.

KING GUSTAV

A good turnout, don't you agree my dear?

QUEEN GUSTAV

They are here for the same reason as you. To see the royal savage swim.

KING GUSTAV

I am assured he is quite tame. And well formed.

QUEEN GUSTAV

So I have heard...Do you see him?

KING GUSTAV

No. But the rest of the Americans are near the starting blocks.

King Gustav turns to his attendant, an impeccably dressed aristocratic gentleman.

KING GUSTAV (CONT'D)

Johan.

JOHAN

Yes sire.

KING GUSTAV

Enquire as to the whereabouts of this Duke of the Sandwich Islands. I wish to see him race.

JOHAN

At once sire.

Johan moves down the bleachers and through the crowd until he addresses the coach of the American swim team.

JOHAN (CONT'D)

Greetings from his highness.

COACH MACK DONAHUGE

Well, say howdy back to his majesty for me!

JOHAN

He wishes to observe the 100 meter race.

COACH MACK DONAHUGE

He's more than welcome too. It's his country ain't it?

JOHAN

His interest is in the Hawaiian. Is he ready to race?

COACH MACK DONAHUGE

Duke? Hell yes! He's around here somewheres.

Mack calls to an Australian swimmer.
COACH MACK DONAHUGE (CONT'D)

Hey Alan! Did Duke come in on the boat with you.

ALAN BOOTH

Not with me mate. That kanaka's probably sawing logs back
on the ship.

Mack looks around counting silently as he finds the other members
of his team.
COACH MACK DONAHUGE

Christ amighty!..Harry!

Harry turns to Mack.
HARRY

Yeah Mack.

COACH MACK DONAHUGE

Did Duke come in on the same boat as you?

HARRY

Nope, I thought he come on earlier, seein how today was the
big race.

Panic in his voice, Mack yells to the crowd around the starting blocks.

COACH MACK DONAHUGE

Anybody here seen Duke this morning?

Blank stares are all he gets in response.

COACH MACK DONAHUGE (CONT'D)

Harry! Duke is probably still on the Finland! You have got to go and fetch him! His race is starting in ten minutes and the gol'dern King of Sweden is waiting to see him swim. Go now as fast as you can and I'll try and delay the start. Go!!

EXT. STREETS OF STOCKHOLM – DAY

Harry, with Pluck at his heels tears off through the crowd, hitches a ride on a wagon headed to the docks, jumps into a skiff and grabs the oars, pulling hard towards the anchored Finland. Securing the skiff he hurtles up the gangplank, then down the deck towards third class.

INT. FINLAND STATEROOMS THIRD CLASS -DAY

Turning the corner into the hallway Harry nearly knocks down Violet Macy, who appears furtive and disheveled.

HARRY

(out of breath) S'cuse me Miss Violet! Have you seen Duke?

VIOLET MACY

Of course not! Why would I?

HARRY

He's late for his race! His majesty the King is a waitin' on him.

Harry turns and races on to his cabin where he bursts into the room.

INT. THIRD CLASS BERTHS – DAY

HARRY

(yelling) Duke! Duke!

Duke sits up in his bunk, slamming his head on the upper berth.

DUKE

Oww! What? What is it.

HARRY

You're sleepin' and the King is waitin' on you! Times a wastin'.

Barefoot,Duke jumps out of the bunk, grabs his shirt and runs out the door with Harry right behind.

EXT. DECK OF THE FINLAND – DAY

Running the length of the ship then jumping into the skiff, Duke grabs the oars as Harry barely makes it aboard.

EXT. ROWBOAT – DAY

HARRY

You reckon I should row Duke? Save yourself for the race?

Duke is rowing with all his considerable strength, the small skiff leaping through the water with each stroke.

DUKE

I just pray we make it in time! I don't know for sure what King's is like in Sweden but back home, the old time kings would knock your head in just for lookin' at em. Let alone keep em waiting. Move with the boat Harry! Help me out!!

DISSOLVE TO:

EXT. WAIKIKI BEACH SPRING 1912 – DAWN

The outline of Diamond head looms in the background as a lithe male body, silhouetted by the sunrise, bends back then uncoils gracefully, tossing a circular fishing net into a turquoise sea. Retrieving the net filled with small tropical fish, he turns as a voice calls.

SARGE

Duke!... Duke! Papa no wait for you.

DUKE

I foget'aready. Help eh?

Two barefoot brothers carry the bulging net at a comfortable trot along a dirt path to a small thatch roofed house. Entering, the dark interior is in sharp contrast to the bright morning sun outside.

INT. KAHANAMOKU HOME – MORNING

The small house is bustling with activity. Dukes father is seated at the kitchen table, wearing his police Captains uniform, a toddler in his lap. Mother brings a bowl of poi and slices of raw onion to the table.

DUKE

Thanks Ma.

Duke and his father take turns dipping their fingers into the bowl, stuffing the gob of poi into their mouths with big bites of onion.

DAD

(between bites) You going swim today?

DUKE

(nodding yes) Uh huh. In the harbor.

DAD

They going pay you?

DUKE

No. It's fo da club. I'm amateur.

DAD

Wat dis amateur? Mean no money?

DUKE

Uh huh. Coach says it means for love. Love of swimming.

DAD

(shaking his head) Love no buy rice. Mo'betta you dive for coins.

DUKE

I will. After.

DAD

Ok. Lets go.

Duke gives his Mom a hug as she hands him two small flour sacks with their lunch then follows his Dad outside the house.
EXT. KAHANAMOKU HOME – DAY

Not speaking, Duke helps his Father hitch an old horse to a small wagon and then climbs up onto the buckboard beside him. Dad slaps the reins on the rump of the horse and they head out, Myna birds squawking and the morning sun flickering through the palm trees along the rutted dirt road.

EXT. HONOLULU HARBOR – MIDDAY

A small group of officious looking middle aged men, use a metal tape to measure a distance alongside the waters edge. A banner announcing "AAU SWIM MEET" hangs flacidly in the windless afternoon. Lounging nearby on barrels and dry docked boats, Duke and his friends goof off, waiting for instructions.

COACH ARNOLD

(hollering to a man with a stopwatch) Are we ready? All right then. Four of you fellers line up here. Now when I fire this pistol, jump in and swim as fast as you can to where Mr. Bishop is standing. Understand? OK, on three. Ready, Steady, BANG!!

As the pistol goes off the four boys dive in staggered succession and begin thrashing towards Mr. Bishop. With no distinct lanes they crash and bump into one another horsing around until one swimmer seemingly rockets away from the pack, swimming until he crosses a rope in the water marking the end of the race. As he crosses, Mr Bishop clicks his stopwatch and then shouts.

MR. BISHOP

Sweet jumpin Jesus!!.. Thomas, come take a look at this.

Coach Arnold and Mr. Bishop walk towards each other meeting at the halfway point along the course. Bishop shows Arnold the stopwatch.

COACH ARNOLD

That can't be right.

MR. BISHOP

Oh, but it is.

COACH ARNOLD

That time is four seconds under the world record Archie.

MR. BISHOP

I told you he was fast.

COACH ARNOLD

You started right at the gun?

MR. BISHOP

Exactly.

COACH ARNOLD

Well, we've got to have him do it again. They'll never believe
it on the mainland.

MR. BISHOP

All right. This time by himself and you take the watch.

COACH ARNOLD

(shouting) Duke!! Come here a minute will ya.

Duke swims over to where the two men stand alongside the swim course.

COACH ARNOLD (CONT'D)

Duke, can you swim the race again? Do you need to rest?

DUKE

Heck no Coach. Let me get the boys.

MR. BISHOP

Just you Duke. We need to calibrate the stopwatch.

DUKE

Sure thing. You going to shoot the gun again?

COACH ARNOLD

Same as before.

DUKE

OK.

Duke swims to the starting point and hauls himself out of the water effortlessly. Coach Arnold takes the stopwatch and goes to the hundred yard mark as Mr. Bishop reloads the starting pistol.

MR. BISHOP

Ready duke?

Duke nods yes.

MR. BISHOP (CONT'D)

(shouting) Ready Thomas?

Coach Arnold waves back.

                    MR. BISHOP (CONT'D)

On my count, Ready, steady, BANG!!

Duke dives cleanly into the water and swims the distance. Coach Arnold clicks the stopwatch and stares in disbelief.

                    COACH ARNOLD

(muttering) Well I'll be a...

Mr. Bishop walks up.

                    MR. BISHOP

What's she say Coach?

                    COACH ARNOLD

New worlds record.

                    MR. BISHOP

That's two new records. The hundred, the two twenty and a tie for the fifty yard freestyle.

                    COACH ARNOLD

Maybe we should measure the distance again.

                    MR. BISHOP

Again? We've checked and double checked. That boy is a bona fide phenomenon and world record holder to boot.

COACH ARNOLD

They're not going to like it on the mainland Archie. Not one bit.

MR. BISHOP

Who cares what they like. The clock doesn't lie. Duke is going to the Olympics.

COACH ARNOLD

(smiling) I guess we better see about getting him some shoes then. If we can find some big enough.

MR. BISHOP

And hide that damn surfboard.

COACH ARNOLD

Amen to that.

DISSOLVE TO:

EXT. STOCKHOLM HARBOR – DAY

The creaking of the oars brings Duke back to the present as he continues to row. Eventually they reach the dock.

HARRY

You go on Duke. I'll see to the boat. I'm right behind you. Go!!

EXT. STREETS OF STOCKHOLM – DAY

Duke jumps out of the skiff and runs through the crowd like a wild man towards the Natatorium. He is halted at the entrance by the Swedish guards.

GUARD 1

(in Swedish) Halt! Halt! What is your business here?

Duke truly looks like a savage. Barefoot and half dressed, a look of panic and fear in his sleep puffed eyes.

DUKE I

..I'm an American! I'm on the team. You've got to let me in!

Seeing his chances of success going down the drain, he pleads with the guards.

DUKE (CONT'D)

Please! Please! Let me in!

A crowd has gathered at the gate to observe this wild native shouting to gain admittance to the stadium. More guards have arrived and are restraining Duke. Abel Kiviat and Alma Richards and Jim Thorpe arrive on the scene, in Olympic uniform.

ABEL KIVIAT

Hey now! Let go! He's with us!

GUARD 2

(in English) And just who are you?

ABEL KIVIAT

We're Americans, that's who! Now let him go and we'll go on inside.

GUARD 2

(in English) You cowboys think we just let Negroes run wild through the streets here?

ALMA RICHARDS

He's not Negro. He's Hawaiian!

ABEL KIVIAT

But so what if he was? We're Americans! You've no right to hold him.

GUARD 2

(in English) I have every right.

The guard signals to restrain the other three athletes.

(in swedish) Place these three under arrest as well.

JIM THORPE

Oh no you don't! It's on now!

More American athletes have arrived and the situation is getting worse by the second.

JOHAN

(in Swedish) Guard!...Guard! In the name of the King release that man.

The guard recognizes Johan.

GUARD 1

(bowing and replying in Swedish) Counselor. This savage was trying to gain entrance. My only concern is the safety of his Majesty.

JOHAN

And he shall be made aware of your excellent attempt. But as we speak, he awaits the appearance of this man. I will take charge of him now. Continue as before.

GUARD 1

(bowing) Counselor.

JOHAN

(in English) Are you the Duke?

DUKE

I'm Duke. Are you the King?

JOHAN

No. But he grows tired of waiting. Let us hasten to the competition.

Thorpe sees that the confrontation is over.

THORPE

Dang it! I thought for sure we was gonna have us a real time of it.

ABEL KIVIAT

Easy there Chief. What happened to (chanting) Smoke that peace pipe, bury that hatchet?

THORPE

I'll smoke if everybody's smokin'.. but I'll tell you what Abel, that tomahawk ain't buried all that deep.

Harry arrives, out of breath as Abel, Thorpe, Alma, Johan and Duke move to enter the Natatorium. The guards have him under arrest..

HARRY

Hey fellers! Wait for me!

Johan turns to see Harry in the arms of the guards.

JOHAN

(to Alma) Is he one of yours?

ALMA RICHARDS

Yep. He's our mascot.

JOHAN

Really?.. Well then, of course he must accompany us.

Johan rolls his eyes and signals to the guard to release Harry. Together they pass through the gates of the Natatorium.

INT. NATATORIUM STOCKHOLM – DAY

The stands have filled since Harry left to retrieve Duke. The King and Queen are in the royal box and the crowd is growing restless. Australian swimmer Alan Booth pleads with the officials.

ALAN BOOTH

C'mon mate. It won't even be a race without the world record holder. Just a few more minutes.

The other competitors in the 100 meter swim are already on the starting blocks as Duke and his friends arrive.

ALAN BOOTH (CONT'D)

Crikey!! Speak of the devil! Here he is now! Hey, Duke! Over here!!

COACH MACK DONAHUE

Where you been boy? The whole world is waitin' on you.

DUKE

(out of breath) Sorry. No one woke me up.

COACH MACK DONAHUE

I'm pretty sure they're not giving out medals for sleepin' son.. Whats her name anyways?

Duke is speechless and averts his eyes.

COACH MACK DONAHUE (CONT'D)

Do you need some time to catch your breath?

DUKE

(sheepishly) No. I'm good to go.

COACH MACK DONAHUE

All right then. Go win one for the US of A.

The officials look up to see if the King has reached the end of his patience, as Johan enters the royal box. The King is looking at his pocket watch, replacing it in his vest at Johan's approach.
                    KING GUSTAV

(in Swedish) Did you find the Duke ?

                    JOHAN

Yes sire. He is ready to race.

                    KING GUSTAV

Ah! There he is now.

As Duke takes his position on the starting block, a swell of applause fills the stadium as the crowd marvels at his physique. Unaware that the applause is for him, he keeps his head down and prepares for the start. An official stands at the starting blocks, his pistol in hand.
                    OFFICIAL 1

(in Swedish) Swimmers at the ready. On my mark....ONE... TWO... BANG!!

The swimmers are away in a staggered start, with Duke no where near the front of the pack. He rapidly makes up lost time, pulling alongside the leaders and then passing them before they reach the fifty meter turnaround. The crowd is cheering wildly as Duke increases his lead. First one body length ahead, then two, plowing through the water he reaches the finish a full two and a half lengths ahead of the nearest competitor. The roar of the crowd is deafening and then grows louder still as the new world record time is announced.
    Dukes teammates, Coach Donahue and Harry surround him.
                    HARRY

You done it Duke!! You done it!!

COACH MACK DONAHUE

Hell of a job son! You can sleep through all your races from now on! Fine by me!

The crowd is hushed as King Gustav stands in his box, his right hand raised to silence the crowd. By the pool Johan has appeared next to Duke.

JOHAN

His highness the King would like you to return to the starting block.

DUKE

He wants me to do it again?

JOHAN

(gesturing toward the blocks) Perhaps. Would you be so kind?

Duke climbs back onto the block in the hushed stadium. King Gustav, extending his arm towards Duke gives a slight bow and then, with his white gloved hands, begins a slow steady clapping. His subjects and then the whole stadium stand and join in the rhythmic clapping. The Champion, an American flag draped across his broad shoulders grins ear to ear and waves back to King and crowd.

FADE TO:

EXT. OLYMPIC STADIUM AWARDS CEREMONY – NIGHT

Athletes from the United States team are in line to receive medals from King Gustav. Alma Richards and Duke Kahanamoku proudly wear their gold medals as the awards ceremony continues. Pop Warner, Colonel Thompson, Count Volkmar, Violet and Baron Macy, Lieutenant and Mrs Patton, Harry and Pluck and the rest of the United States contingent stand in the bleachers looking on.

ANNOUNCER

(in Swedish) For the United States...1500 meter relay. Silver medal, Abel Kiviat.

Abel steps forward and the King places the medal around his neck.

ANNOUNCER (CONT'D)

For the United States...Decathlon and Pentathlon...Gold medals, James Thorpe.

POP WARNER

(aside to Colonel Thompson) If he can keep his mouth shut just this once.

KING GUSTAV

From his excellency the Czar of Russia.

Jim steps forward and King Gustav presents him with a large solid gold replica of a Viking ship.

KING GUSTAV (CONT'D)

From the people of Sweden.

The King is handed a second large gold trophy which he passes on to Jim.

Thorpe, with both hands full is straining to hold the weighty trophies. His majesty seems to move in exaggerated slow motion as he places one, then another solid gold medal around Jim's neck. Once again the King raises his gloved hand to silence the packed stadium. Seeing that Thorpe is straining under the heavy load, the King smiles.

KING GUSTAV (CONT'D)

You sir, are the greatest athlete in the world.

JIM THORPE

(pausing for just a moment) Thank's King.

Laughter is immediate from the Americans then, as the translation of Thorpes reply makes it's way around the stadium, waves of laughter fill the air and the crowd rises to it's feet in a standing ovation.

EXT. NEW YORK CITY- MADISON AVENUE- DAY

Streets and buildings overflow with well wishers welcoming home the Olympic team. The sun is all but obscured by the deluge of confetti and streamers tossed from towering skyscrapers lining the parade route. Harry Naughton sits with Pluck in his lap between Hawaiian champion Duke Kahanamoku and Colonel Thompson in an open car, waving to the crowd.

HARRY NAUGHTON

Ain't this just grand Colonel?

COLONEL THOMPSON

Yes Harry, and well deserved. We have blazed a trail that many after us can follow with pride...It's been a fantastic journey for you Harry. What do you consider your fondest memory?

## HARRY NAUGHTON

That's a hard one Colonel. I guess meeting the King and his missus and going to the palace would have to take the cake... Don't see much chance of repeatin' that one... What do you reckon his majesty is doin right this minute?

## COLONEL THOMPSON

I suspect Harry, if he's anything like me, that after the guests have gone... he has the servants count the spoons.

As the confetti falls and the cheers recede Harry smiles and waves.

## FADE TO BLACK

# EPILOGUE

## JIM THORPE

In the fall, Jim Thorpe returned to the Carlise Indian school in Pennsylvania. Coached by Glenn Scobey "Pop" Warner, he was again selected for the 1912 All America team. In a highly publicized game against Army, future President Dwight "Ike" Eisenhower would permanently injure his knee, attempting, alongside West point classmate Omar Bradley, to disable Thorpe. Within a year he would be stripped of his Olympic medals. Playing small town baseball for miniscule amounts of money disqualifying him from amateur athletics forever. The most famous and highest salaried athlete of his era, he excelled at professional baseball and football, in later years spearheading the formation of what would become the National Football league. His medals and Olympic records restored posthumously, he was voted Athlete of the 20th century by the United States Congress.

## DUKE KAHANAMOKU

Duke remained the indisputable champion of swimming for over twenty years.

As ambassador of the sport and his beloved Hawaii, he traveled the globe, giving swimming and diving exhibitions. Introducing the "forbidden" sport of surfing, he hand shaped surfboards from planks of wood found at local lumber yards, amazing thousands of fans with his truly Olympian water skills. Competing and winning medals in four separate Olympiads, his legacy is that of the true amateur.

## AVERY BRUNDADGE

Avery was destined to be forever eclipsed by superior athletes Jim Thorpe and Alma Richards during his athletic career. Thought by many to be instrumental in the discovery of Thorpes professionalism, he was, as President of the International Olympic Committee in later years, adamant that his medals and records not be reinstated.

## "POP" WARNER

Coach of the Carlisle Indian school and numerous Ivy league colleges over his career, his legacy lives on through the Pop Warner football programs found in every corner of the United States.

## GEORGE S PATTON

Placing fifth overall in the modern pentathlon, Patton's decision to use the larger 38 caliber pistol ultimately cost him the Gold medal. Selected to represent the United States again in 1916, the war in Europe shelved the games and he was instead ordered to Mexico in pursuit of Pancho Villa. Serving under General 'Black Jack' Pershing, he pioneered the use of motorized cavalry using automobiles to capture several of Villas lieutenants. World War I found him once again serving under General Pershing in Europe, acquiring the tactical tank training that would distinguish him in the subsequent world war as Americas most successful General.

## HARRY NAUGHTON

No record of the intrepid stowaway's future exploits exist. We can only hope that his adventure with these Titans of the 20th century instilled a sense of sportsmanship and brotherhood that served him well for the remainder of his life. His loyal companion Pluck, seems to have made an indelible impression on the future General Patton who chose as companion and guardian of his children, that same breed of pointy nosed English pit bull.

S. S. FINLAND LEAVING NEW YORK HARBOR

WGA REGESTRATION # 1266994
Email: burrastontim@yahoo.com
Phone: # 760-473-8374